Me and the Fat Man

JULIE MYERSON

HARPER PERENNIAL
London, New York, Toronto and Sydney

Harper Perennial
An imprint of HarperCollins*Publishers*
77–85 Fulham Palace Road
Hammersmith
London W6 8JB

www.harperperennial.co.uk

This edition published by Harper Perennial 2005
1

First published in Great Britain by Fourth Estate 1998

A catalogue record for this book
is available from the British Library

This novel is entirely a work of fiction. The names,
characters and incidents portrayed in it are the work of the
author's imagination. Any resemblance to actual persons,
living or dead, events or localities is entirely coincidental.

ISBN 0 00 720297 0

Typeset in Plantin by Avon Dataset Ltd, Bidford on Avon

Printed and bound in Great Britain by Clays Ltd, St Ives plc

For Ruth Picardie

One

I sat on a damply green bench in the Garden for the Blind and waited for a man to come, just as one always did.

The longer you waited, the stiller you sat, the closer he might be likely to come.

At first he might be going out of his way to look head-down in a hurry or else he'd perhaps be coming through the black, little swing gate from Quiet Street, either as a short cut to the main city road or else on his way to the NCP car park where the red lit-up sign always said Full.

Maybe he'd slow and stop off at the gents' toilets – a longish, dirty-looking building with the sign hanging off and dark hedges all around. But you could count on him not being long in there – I never got over how efficient in and out he'd be. After, he'd go more slowly – relieved, looking around him. Maybe he'd stop for a second to light a fag, then looking up, pretending – like they all do – not to see me, coming over slow and lazy to sit on the bench.

Hiya, you'd want to say. But you didn't. You looked coolly ahead, like you never spoke to strangers. Why would you?

Making out he didn't know I was there or didn't care, he might have a briefcase or he might not. He might just have a plastic carrier, crinkled and blackened from so much regular using.

This one carried no bag, nothing. He had on a dark

green parka thing with some orange flashes and what I took to be a sports motif of two spears and a flame. Newish trainers and a brand-new leather dog lead – the plaited sort – but no dog.

Lost your dog? I queried softly.

No – he stuttered a bit, No, I haven't.

And he looks over at me – just a quickish glance, eyebrows lifted, then away again, a look which scorches. He isn't half as old as I'd have thought from faraway, but he's ratty enough. Clean nails, but dirty hands, black in the cracks like a garage man.

The wind blows and air rushes fast around us, leaves lifting and then down. Dust and grit sprayed against your legs.

He takes out some fags, pointing the crushed packet at me. I pull one and as he moves in to give me a light, I accidentally whiff his breath – an hour of boozing and not much time with a toothbrush.

Holding the cigarette between my lips, I unzip my jacket and get out my hair, a twisted scrap of a tail but freshly washed this morning and blonde, how they like it. If it goes fuzzy – excitement, sweat, the rain – I damp it down with gel, the green, sweet-shop smelling one. Sometimes I plait it, pull it off my face: there are hygiene rules for work, which is fair enough.

Now, I pull off the laggy band with the two plastic bobbles that clack. Let it loose – swuff, swuff – wait for him to react.

He glances at the part of my neck just before it divides into chest. What's he seeing? Flat little girl to spoil in a cotton vest? Or busty woman's tits, squashy as fruit and good for kicking around?

Have a good look, I say.

I take a thick mouthful of smoke, get rid of it slowly. He makes a good show of laughing, for a nervous man.

You're not showing me much, he goes.

How much do you want?

What're you offering?

You want to go somewhere?

He looks away and laughs like he doesn't believe it or like it always happens to him, both. And when his eyes come back, they're not messing any more.

Like where?

I've got a place.

Your place?

Someone else's.

How much?

As usual, I make up the amount, the most money I dare say. I used to play at shops with Sally – lining up tins from the cupboards, making up what amount you like 'cause the money (heavy, dirty old money) wasn't real.

Now, the money's still unreal. Sometimes you make up a big amount, for the fun of seeing them react. Sometimes – blonde hair, flash of tit, lovely, softly willing girl – you get it.

He winds the dog lead round his hand, then lets it untwist slowly. OK, he says.

The room was too hot and it stank of people's eggy breath and old undies, not mine I might add. Normally I was in the other one, the front one that was cleaner and had twice the light, but today it was unavailable – you knew this because it was shut with a chair and a cardboard box pulled over in front of it.

Mara took the key away if you didn't pay – that or got her maid to hassle you even if you were with a punter. Fair enough. If you were making it, you could afford the rent. But she made allowances for me. Why? I don't know, maybe she liked me. I was the youngest, the blondest, the best figure, the least used. I was married so she considered me clean. I got the rooms on a one-off basis – hour at a time, so long as there was one free. No one else knew this of course; Mara was good in that way.

He was quiet, fairly polite, keen to get on with it. I was glad when he put the dog lead down.

I don't have a dog, he went as I unzipped him, I just like the feel of this, know what I mean?

I said nothing. They don't expect you to make speeches, wouldn't hear them if you did.

Talking about the dog lead had done its job, made him hard.

I've not done this before, he said, eyeing the right angle between cock and groin.

Like hell, I thought. He clocked the Durex and said, I'd pay you a tenner more without and I told him to shut up, I was in charge.

He made a little click in his throat and, as I unrolled a Durex and eased it on, he coughed to hide how much he was aroused. The rubbery odour hid the fish stink of his cock, a smell which'd lodge in the rough, screwy hairs at the base. I'd learned to hold my breath and turn my imagination off while I was doing it.

It was all over in less than a minute.

I wiped my fingers on a Kleenex. When I got home, I'd have a good rinse with medicated mouthwash.

He left, the dog lead slapping in his bum pocket. I checked the money was still where I'd put it. I went straight to the Nationwide and added it to my fund.

It had been a long fucking winter and I was sick and tired of running around with other people's coat collars sticking up my nose. Plus Mervyn the second chef was getting a fixation on me and it was starting to piss me off. That and then Auntie's passing away half-way through a shift.

Auntie wasn't anyone's real auntie, we just called

her that. She'd been at Greenaway's since forever, folding napkins and sorting linen at the top of those stairs.

That morning she just toppled and by the time she reached the bottom step she wasn't alive anymore. I'd never seen a dead person unless you count my mother dragged out of the sea, which I don't remember.

And then he walked in.

A man well past middle-age, he's the clever, disorganised type – messy, wearing-out clothes – but he doesn't fool me. You can tell he's comfortably off, went to a posh school and all that. Well-off is a funny thing. You get billionaires who look like tramps – who walk around with grease pouring off their hair, who hide the clues like it's a game. It's as if they can't help it. Give them a bit of education and they let their nails go black. Maybe I'm exaggerating, but the basic point is true.

I haven't booked, he says, leaning forward and spreading cleanish fingers on the fireside table. Any chance of a table for one?

No problem, I tell him because we're quiet today – I don't even have to check the book – which is lucky considering we've just killed a member of staff. I ask him if he'd like a drink upstairs first – they usually do – and I glance in and see that Paula's laying up as fast as she can. We're behind with everything.

He says he would. Like a drink.

We walk up the brown-coloured stairs with the gold rods reflecting and he must have got to me already in some way because I'm seeing it all through his eyes – the wall-lights which are sheaves of golden wheat with the bulb poking through, paintings of uncooked food like garlic and onions and berries all up the wall and the stencils of spatulas and serving spoons and sharp knives as you go down again.

5

You're not local, are you? he says, and I jump – I'm in a state, to tell the truth.

Your accent, he goes, It's not from round here.

I tell him I used to be in London, but I moved down last year. Why bother to tell the whole truth to strangers?

Lovely city, he says, I've been here forever myself.

I take a look at him then. He's oldish. The stubble of a beard pokes redly through his pale skin, but the hair on his head is almost white. As he rubs his hands together, a signet ring slips around on the joint.

We'll need the table back at two-fifteen, I tell him.

Fine by me.

I hand him the menu, then try to light the fire, which is always a pain to do.

Your hand's shaking, he points out and I confess to him that I'm all over the place since we had a majorly fatal accident just over an hour ago.

Oh, he goes, probably just thinking I mean someone's nicked their finger or scalded theirselves or the equivalent.

Downstairs, I tell him, turning the gas tap, each fucking match going out. Someone who works here. Worked, I should say.

Want a hand?

Don't worry – the fake logs catch at last and the fake flames lick. I rock back on my heels.

What sort of an accident? he says.

Actually (as I speak I'm noticing ash on the carpet and next to his elbow a dish of spat-out olive stones from last night) someone fell downstairs and died.

No! – he's so shocked.

Mmm, just now, yeah. It's awful.

I shrug to show how tough I am and then I look full into his eyes and I can't help it, like an idiot I burst out laughing.

★

I'd started taking the men in the summer so I suppose you could have said it was a recent thing.

Some people might be judgemental. They might think it's weird, a perverted activity, because I wasn't broke and I wasn't even single – why sell yourself, when you've a man to bring home money? – and that was on top of my quite reasonable wage every week from Greenaway's.

At the time of starting I told myself a crowd of things. My mother had not exactly kept her body to herself (so my foster parents enjoyed reminding me) so why not me and for some return? It was the thrill that got me going, but it was the money also – secret money, quick as a flash money, money that was all mine.

Because my mind doesn't have to go where my body goes. My soul isn't in my mouth – but plenty of men would pay good money to be in there.

I'm a nice, well-balanced girl, I told myself, a girl in search of a better life. I can't wait at table and carry coats forever. I'm twenty-seven, nice-looking. I've never minded sex and I've never had money of my own, not notes coming into your pocket quicker than they drift out – not so much that you could throw the notes up in the air and they'd flutter down around your head.

You could whack men off for that sort of money – a few quick flicks of the wrist – whereas you'd have to do a job for years and the money would just slow-drip into your hands like Chinese torture, so limited and mean it slips away between your fingers before you've had any pleasure from it.

This way you get to feel the notes, the fatness of them, the warm heaviness of coin in your purse. It's for me, this money – and anyway, the truth is it gets easy once you've done it a few times – you learn to put away the disgust. A person can get used to anything: think of undertakers, or those poor fuckers at the scene of the crime, or medical students.

So you pluck them from that park, take them, take their money, let them go again. They're nothing to me, these men, their hearts bumping away in their jackets as they lose themselves. I could cut their dicks off if I wanted. How do they know I don't carry a knife? Their heads are back in ignorance and ecstasy and all I see is the apple bobbing in their fine, white flesh. In the end they're gone and only the money's left behind.

It's not their fault. I don't blame them. I blame the hormones and the loneliness of the nine to five. The cold journey to work, the paper to shuffle, the ads with the panties or the tits in them. With me they get a chance to bloom and overflow.

And I don't do anything funny, just blow or hand relief and always with protection. The more they want it, the quicker it is. Sometimes I'll be in and out of there in five minutes flat, maybe seven. Sometimes I'll be lighting a fag and sipping a coffee less than ten minutes after.

It's the shock, he said. Relax and let it all come out.

I gasped, wiped my eyes with a tea towel.

It seems bad to laugh, I told him. Because now even though I was laughing, the muscles in my face were indicating they wanted to switch over and cry.

It's quite OK, he said – as if women cracked up in front of him all the time.

He leaned his head back against the hump of the sofa. His look was level and calm. He linked his fingers one by one, like a game.

His eyes were the sort you can't see into but you know there's lots going on. I don't know what he was saying but I let his voice into my head like it was music or sleep.

I'm OK now, I told him, and I was.

I went behind and pulled up the blinds and sun made the room nicer. I removed the dish of olive stones, not that it seemed to bother him, but it was bothering me.

You're a nice girl, aren't you? he said.

I laughed.

You seem nice anyway.

Can I tell you the specials? I said and I began on the pan-fried halibut with salsa verde.

You must meet Gary, he said, interrupting.

Gary?

My – well – you'd love him. He'd love you.

I looked at him. Your what? I said.

What?

Who's Gary?

There was some intimacy between us, so it seemed OK to be direct. But, truthfully, I was torn between wanting to know and wanting to go through what was cooked fresh that day. All those specials were lodged in my head just waiting to spill out.

He's my lodger, he said.

Why do I have to meet him?

He laughed. Amy, he said, Oh Amy –

I must have looked gone out at him, because he said, OK, poor girl, I'll come clean. I recognised you as soon as I walked in and I'm still in shock, I can't believe it – it's like seeing her again, seeing Jody. I knew your mother. Last time I saw you, you were stark naked on the island, cracking pine nuts with a little round stone.

At school, they made you write your life story. Mine was pretty short and sweet.

9

I was born on the island of Eknos to a teenager called Jody, who drowned when I was six. Jody was from St Albans. She didn't really speak to me. My father might have been English too – or Greek or German. Maybe American. It's true I reckon that Jody fucked nearly everyone that stepped off that ferry boat.

Jody's parents had said they wanted no more to do with her so, after she died, I was given to foster parents in London.

In the school essay I didn't say about the fucking. I wanted to be normal like all the navy blue girls, so I didn't put anything much. I said I had a Dad called Brian and a Mum called Eileen and that Brian had a beard and Eileen had red marks where her bra straps rubbed.

When people aren't your parents, you see them more clearly.

When I was seven I was taken to see a man for the express purpose of talking about Jody. My mum, she had a fascination. Grown-ups still got excited or cross when they talked about her when I was out of the room – you knew because the sounds changed as you opened the door.

The man held my shoulders too tightly and asked me to think of the island and tell him what I saw.

I saw nothing and he was truly narked.

Try and concentrate, Amy, he said. How do you feel when I talk about your mother?

Bad? I guessed.

He opened a sweet out of its wrapper – lovely, acidy smell. He deliberately turned it over in his hand so I could see it had a pink side and a green side. There was blurring where the colours touched. He said I could have it when the session was over.

I chewed my fingers with my front teeth but he tutted and pulled my hands from my face.

Uh huh, he went. Bad.

Eileen looked at Brian. Brian looked away, then down, then back at the man.

Amy, said the man quite loudly like he wanted everyone to hear, Why do you chew your fingers when I talk about your mother?

I did not speak.

Eileen sighed. She had little red veins down the sides of her nose, like a cold wind had been rushing past her all her life. I put down my fingers and tried to chew the inside of my face. They all watched me. They made out that they knew what I was doing.

Eileen is dead and buried now and Brian and my foster-sister Sally are not important in this story. They say life's a series of choices, but I don't know. So far it's always been other people doing things to me – marrying me, signing papers which decided my life, pissing me off and so on.

If you knew how hard we work on your behalf, Brian said, teeth gritted. If it had been a movie, he'd have grabbed my collar, held my face up to his in the grainy shadows. As it was he went on peeling his boiled egg, pulling off the white membrane and shell with fingernails he filed to a point at traffic lights. It was unusual for a man to file his nails. Brian – who said the poor should all be forced to get sterilised – was very exact in this way.

Sometimes I relaxed and forgot to eat the skin of my hands and the old world popped up: old men moving things in corners, a slick of salt on your skin and the friendly warmth between my thighs – her hair, yellow as custard and twice as creamy.

Her hair, I said, A big thing of long hair.

Eileen nodded at the man to show I was remembering right, that my mother had that hair. I flushed. I had managed to make up the truth.

The man was medically trained. He made us all a cup of tea.

Eileen said I must have been remarkable there, with my so pale face and long pale hair.

Eknos: a postcard in my head of an unreal place – a coloured snap of blues, wide seas and so on where other people go. Trees so herbal and foreign they're almost black, starved cats asleep on tables and rabbits who sit on wire mesh so their droppings fall on the ground, no mess.

The rabbits are kept for eating not as pets, so no one minds. I sit under the pee-smelling hutches and squidge the droppings in my fingers – poor rabbits, waiting for her to come out of there where she's been a long time. The men roar up on bikes – shout things, bare hairy arms holding on. They straddle me on the bike and show me how to move the gears, but my feet don't touch. Bike wobbles. She catches me – suddenly there – and we go inside. We belong together, me and my barely-remembered shape of a mother.

Which reminds me, her shape: tall and skinny with breasts that jut out suddenly – a roof over my head. Then, her belly, growing fast, her amazing belly button – upended and pale brown like the uncracked top of an egg. Her rolling up, tongue licking, lighting up. Her hair a wide, far curtain – shutting me off from the sky's dazzle when I go to sleep in her shadow.

In the olive trees, a blue painted chair is stuck upside down and the tree stumps have paper bags over them. In winter the sea roars below us. Months of just her smell, her vague touch, nothing else.

*

12

I didn't know Auntie's last name, but I daresay Hetty had it for the wage slips.

She was about eighty – I mean it – and yet she still put on eye-shadow so thick and shiny it went into her eyebrows. She cared for that linen like she was the only person in the world who could do the job, but any of us could have sorted it in half the time.

A cab dropped her at the same time every morning. She changed out of her boots and into elasticated pumps and a wrap-around nylon apron with racehorses round it. All morning she'd be perched on her stool at the top of that steep rake of stairs facing the airing cupboard.

She sat there for two hours taking the fresh napkins out, cutting the plastic tape and folding them. She kept a half-pint beer glass topped up with cooking sherry in the cupboard and was pretty pissed by the time she left at twelve.

She liked to try and talk to Jack about sex.

Bet you broke a few hearts, eh Auntie? he went, dropping calf's kidneys in a pan to sizzle. She bunched up her old lips, trying to hide how hungry she was for him to say this. Yes, she said, she'd have to admit that she was, but she wasn't going to start telling him all about it, and anyway God loved her now.

When Jack laughed and his head went back, you saw the little thing at the back of his throat waving, pinkly wet.

Auntie was planning on getting the fare together for the jumbo jet to Australia to visit her niece – God willing, she always said – but as far as we could tell she'd been saving for years and wasn't likely to go now, so you have to assume God wasn't all that keen on the idea.

Paula said she died with her mouth and eyes wide open and that she went to the toilet all over the floor. Sometimes, when I think of how people enter this

13

world all pale and soft and clean – and then how they die in their own mess, I can't find anything good in it.

Jack said everyone could help themselves to a stiff drink from the bar. My guess is Mervyn guzzled more than one.

Then, it was back to work like after a fire practice – on with the show. People were booked and there was no question of cancelling. A party of ten Japanese delegates was due at one-fifteen. It was how Auntie would've wanted it and I'm not being funny.

No one knew Jody – that was or is the nature of Jody – so it's hard to take in that he says he knew her.

Hello Amy, he goes again, just dropping out the name like it totally belongs to him. My face hots up at hearing my name said like that.

There's a bit of a silence and at last he says, Ever go to the Garden for the Blind in Henrietta Park?

Why? I flush.

Haven't I seen you there?

I look at his shabby tracksuit bottoms, deck shoes, a shirt hanging untucked around his waist, a thick jersey that's gone thicker in the wash. He is at least sixty and I know I'd have remembered him if I'd done him. He wears one of those creepy copper bracelets you see in the ads.

I think of the Garden for the Blind, the bench with the badly-done heart scratched on, the litter bin crammed with Lilt cans and old nappies, the smoky flower beds, the dregs of the day, the men, my men.

No, I say, I don't think I know it. You must be thinking of someone else.

I take his grey coat flung on the sofa and slide the hanger into the shoulders, catch the sweetish whiff of old sweat from the satin lining.

I'm pretty certain of this, he says. It's that hair. You're pretty hard to miss, you know.

I shrug. I've never even heard of it, I tell him.

He seems amused. He flicks the pages of the wine list without looking at them.

I'm sorry, he says and he's smiling now. It's just the most incredible coincidence, scarcely believable.

My silence makes him look up as I knew it would.

How did you know her? I ask him.

Join me, he says, Have a drink.

I can't, sorry.

Another time?

The clock chimes twelve, time for Auntie's cab. I wonder whether anyone has thought of cancelling it or if it will just turn up as per normal.

Do you like your job? he asks me.

I shrug. It's work.

I ask him what he fancies to drink and he says a Kir. I polish up the rim of the glass really hard. Last night's dirty coffee cups are still in the sink.

Look Amy, he says, I'll level with you. Jody wasn't just a friend. She was the biggest and best thing in my life for a while. There are things I'd like to tell you, things I'd like to ask you. Could we be friends? I'd like to have some time, get to know you. Could we meet somewhere, talk?

Oh, I say, A date is it?

He laughs and then looks sad.

There isn't a lot of time, I tell him, Generally.

I take him his wine, dry roasted nuts in a pottery dish. He raises his glass – To you, he says.

How did you know her?

It's a long story.

Where should we meet?

Paula comes up the back staircase with the lemons and we both look at her. The smell of her hand cream smudges the air after she's gone.

He says could we meet in the Garden for the Blind

15

and I say I don't think so. He starts saying how it's got all these rare plants – all the names written out in braille – and I say I'm sure it has, but –

It's very private, he goes.

Oh what, I say, Because no one can see you?

He laughs.

I don't know the place, I say again, Why there? Why go on about it?

He picks up yesterday's *Gazette* off the table and starts to read. I hope we can be friends, he says without looking up. I'm Harris.

Harris what?

Just Harris.

He has some numbers scribbled in blue biro on his palm like a kid. His wrist is so pale and hairless I could bite into it.

The first man I sucked for money was Guy Carroll, an old school chum of my husband's.

He called me up at work the day after we met at some party and took me out to lunch. Behind my husband's back – secret, smoochy. Our date was at his club. My husband had been to a posh school but was the type to wear scuffed jackets and deny his background. Guy was the opposite type. He had banker's hair – tight, wiry, terrier curls that seemed stuck on to his head. He stood stiffly to attention and wore cufflinks and there was a mass of blackheads at the back of his neck you longed to squeeze.

I ate three courses, keeping up with him.

Not fussed about your figure then? he said, and you could tell it was what he thought you said to a woman.

He talked loudly, always looking straight ahead. As his mouth opened, you saw the meat going greyer and softer. Now and then he wiped his mouth or edged his wrist out of the cuff to see the time. The waiters came

16

back and forward, asking how the meal was and topping up the wine. I gave one a look, to show it was all a pretence with Guy.

He told me stuff about his time as an officer in the army – he was thick as shit – he was a banker now. I didn't know what I was doing there really or what was going on – only that he kept this permanent smirk on his face, like we both knew something we weren't owning up to.

You don't like me, he said suddenly, his face flushed with the triumph of working it out.

Oh, I lied, You're OK.

What don't you like? His eyes lit up with accusing greenish flecks.

Well, all right, you're an asshole, I said.

He seemed pleased by this. What else, gorgeous?

You're so fucking uptight, middle-aged.

He closed his eyes. Am I?

You think you're so great because you've got money.

Money. Have I? What else?

Nothing else.

Oh come on, he went, There must be something else.

I was liking this game. It was like holding the zapper for the TV, changing channels whether the programme was boring or not, just for the sound of the click.

Back at his hotel, he rolled on a Durex and I let him put it in my mouth. The TV was on with the sound turned down and it was Crufts. I love dogs so I propped a pillow under my head and watched out of the corner of my eye and it took my mind off the stretching of my lips and the sour throbbing as his dick rimmed thickly up and down.

You like doggies? he asked me when he'd come and the little teat at the end was hot and full.

I do, I told him straight, I'd like to breed and show them.

He laughed. My husband and I had a sheepdog, Megan, but she was his really, not mine. I felt no particular love for her and she always went to him in preference to me, even when I was the one who fed her.

I continued to watch the screen, but Guy seemed to want me out. He disposed of the rubber and tucked his prick back in his boxers. A Lurcher was going to win, I just knew it. Then, as he pulled up his trousers, he put his hand in his pocket and pulled out three new, pinkish notes fresh from the bank.

What's this? I said.

For your trouble, Sweetie Pie.

Posh git, I thought, and I was going to throw it back at him but then I thought about being in a shop with it in my hands, what it could buy. Take it, a calm, retail voice whispered to me.

OK, I said, and put it in my bag. He watched me slip it in the money pocket and do up the zip. He saw me, still watching the dogs on the TV and so calmly taking his money and he licked his lips which were already moist.

After that we met now and then, until he got posted abroad. He left a biggish hole which it was tempting to fill, so one day I went down the Garden for the Blind and did.

It was the beginning of lunch, two or three days after the visit from Harris. I'd done the cold table and wiped down and was rolling a quick cigarette at the kitchen bar when Paula said someone was asking for me.

I swigged my soda. Who?

Paula shrugged. A couple of chaps.

Which table?

There's only the one in.

Reluctantly, I put down the ciggy.

18

Jack was finishing the duck confit as I went past but we hadn't been told all the specials yet or even done the board. I went out there. A cloud of dust turning over and over in the low sunshine and you could smell the newish carpets. It was the Harris bloke, sitting reading the paper with a youngish and pretty ugly-porky bloke next to him.

He beamed at me like I'd just said something so witty.

I told you I'd bring Gary, he said.

Gary and Amy. Amy and Gary. Gary and Amy and Harris. And Jimmy. Jimmy. Your life clouds over and your heart contracts when you say these names.

Gary was about thirtyish and there was no way round it, he was fat. He was very fat – I mean, he had a fatness problem. I'd certainly remember if I'd done him, though I imagine you'd have to root around in all that flesh to find the shrimp that was his dick and then you'd suffocate in all that thickness. Small, dark eyes and brownish skin and black hair. A big head and little angel-boy lips – chubby hands, thick thighs that strained at his trousers and a floppy brown cord jacket. With his eyes half-closed he looked like he didn't want to be anywhere at all and especially not here.

I couldn't help it, I was staring at him, he was such an eyeful.

Harris had shaved so his face was smooth and pale all over and he had on new-looking clothes. In fact, he looked like some hard-arse TV personality – full of shiny clues and jokes, a bit handsome and a bit cocky.

This is Amy, Harris told him. What a miracle, eh? I still can't believe it. I just walked in and there she was.

So you said, Gary said.

So say hi, the older man told him.

Hi, said Gary.

19

He barely looked at me, total lack of interest. I tried to judge the relationship, wondering if they were a couple – there was a slight, loose, softness about the fat man. But I somehow couldn't see Harris in bed with a bloke. I put down some bread and brought menus, and they fidgeted about a bit and ordered a bottle of Saumur and I went away.

In the kitchen, Karen was writing up the specials. The hair at the back of her neck had been done with a razor – made you want to stroke her like a pet.

Well, who was it? said Paula.

No one, I told her, putting the wine order on the spike.

In the back, Mervyn tried to talk to me about his sex problems. Fuck off, I said and I didn't care what he thought or if someone heard me.

You're no fun, he said, heaving open the metal door of the cold store with his shoulder, glancing around for cream buckets. I went back to the bar and got out the wine. I lit my cigarette and took a puff but it went out, so I left it till after I'd dealt with Harris.

I set the ice bucket on a stand, opened the wine with some difficulty and gave him a drop to taste.

You live with him? I said to Gary.

He shrugged. More or less, he went.

Come round to lunch, said Harris.

I don't know – I began, but he whipped a piece of paper out of his pocket and wrote on it.

I won't take no for an answer, he said. It's extraordinary, to see you again – I believe it was meant to happen. I mean it, Amy. I've found you; I can't just let you slip away.

I looked to see Gary's reaction to all this, but he immediately glanced off in a bored way. His arse took up the space of two persons on the banquette.

Sunday? Harris passed me the paper with the

address and a phone number and I stashed it in my apron pocket. One-ish? he said.

I said, Fine. What harm could it do? I hadn't had so much excitement in a long time.

Harris ordered the pan-fried scallops on a bed of noodles and seaweed, the grilled salmon with lime and broad bean sauce to follow, Gary the pepper risotto. Maybe he was vegetarian. You get some fat ones.

Upstairs, Hetty was interviewing for someone to replace Auntie. She lined us up and told us not to mention Auntie's fatal accident, then Jack pointed out that it had already been in the fucking *Gazette*.

Let's just get the job filled, Hetty snapped, Then we can worry about what's been reported where.

The air was thick with upset and whisperings, but they needn't have worried, none of the applicants seemed to know about Auntie. Hetty brought them round the kitchens one by one and nobody looked up at the top of the stairs in a gruesome way. Some even stood innocently on the actual spot where she'd died and all they asked were questions about rota and sick leave.

In the toilet, I blew my nose and took a good look at my two eyes in the mirror. I'd got the brownish eye pencil too close in and it gave me a shifty look. I tore off a bit of toilet paper and removed it, then licked my lips to make them wet-look.

Then I sat on the closed lid and stared at the piece of paper. The address meant nothing to me, was in a part of the city I'd heard of but never been. The writing was fancy and girlish, with the number seven crossed in a French way. I looked at it a long time and then I put it away and went back out.

Who're your friends? Karen went, when I shouted

out the order to Mervyn, making sure not to go anywhere near him.

What friends? I was getting sick of all the fuss. I spooned *aïoli* into a ramekin to go with a prawns Paula was about to take.

The two guys who keep on looking at you. The big dark one and the thin old one.

I don't know them, I said and went out of my way to yawn.

You have to realise, if you have a baby when you're still a kid yourself, you won't know how to look after it, you'll lose your temper sometimes, you won't be the ideal kind of parent.

Jody had left St Albans at sixteen and hitched around Europe with Justin Appleby. Just like that. Left school, home, parents and all for this guy. I never met Justin, but her whisperings about him live in my head. He had long, matted hair and a laid-back outlook and he took drugs and lived off the state because of his ideals. Even years later, it was Justin this and Justin that. She was crazy about him and her parents had the bad grace to call him an unwashed layabout.

Even now, when I think of Justin being sneered at, his personal hygiene criticised, it tears me up. When she ran away travelling with Justin, her father said he wouldn't leave her any money but she said, What's money? We wanted to travel the world and we wanted a kid.

I close my eyes and I see the two of them on a ferry headed somewhere, her head buried in the meaty darkness of his afghan coat, his black hair apache-sleek – and it just about slays me to think that the baby they're dreaming of isn't me.

They argued in Lausanne. He tore the gold plate hoop earring from her lobe and it needed three stitches. He picked up his bedroll and she never saw him again.

The day she got off the ferry at Kapsali, it was raining and four dogs were doing it on the quay, one on top of the other like stacking chairs.

Two

My husband said, Did you know it's pissing down outside?

I didn't. I was still towelling my hair and wondering whether to bother with the drier.

I'm going in, he told me, swigging the last of his coffee, I've got a meeting at half nine. I can drop you if you want.

I said yes to his generous offer and hurried up with applying shadow on my lids and under my lower lashes and finishing off with mascara. As he watched me he went moody and quiet. He didn't like it when I put on makeup. He knew nothing of my little hobby, but he didn't trust the way I looked and I guess at the end of the day he was right.

Last night we'd had sex, oh yes, but you wouldn't think it to look at us now. You wouldn't think I'd had my legs around him and him kissing my breasts and saying darling and all that. For us, sex led to nothing – that's the way it was with us. We could fuck, speak, eat from the same fridge, but nothing we did lined up any more. We could come together, make sparks and then be miles apart again. Nights and days were all split up from each other – good and bad, close or angry. We'd divided them like we'd divided ourselves.

He picked his papers up off the table and fiddled with his earring – his two fingers at computer software salesmanship. But I need to go by twenty to, he said. Is the dog fed?

She is.

Megan lifted her chin at the word 'dog' – or was it just his worshipped voice? – then sighed it back down on to her paws. She whimpered softly and I whispered shut up just low enough so he wouldn't hear. I looked at the kitchen clock and it said just gone half past.

I heard him cleaning his teeth upstairs, spitting, rinsing, flushing – familiar sounds, sliding past me and into nothing. He believed himself a free spirit with his dog and his earring and his job driving all over the place in a denim jacket, but he did everything just when he should.

Three years we'd been married and more than ever it was a marriage of convenience. It's convenient for him and it's occasionally convenient for me, I told Paula.

We laughed, but it was getting to be not that funny anymore. I had lots of married life jokes and I saved them up for work.

Oh, he's not that bad, Paula would go, picking at her feet under the table. Maybe she secretly fancied him. He was the kind of man other women secretly fancied. He seemed impressive until you got up close.

In the car going down Milmont I said something about Auntie and he snapped at me.

You hardly knew her, he said, as if I was faking it.

We worked together, I cried. She was an old lady.

You laughed at her.

I know, I said, But I never wished for her to break her skull.

These things happen. Maybe she's better off, he said and I knew he was thinking of his own mum and her Alzheimer's.

By the way, I said lightly, I'm out this Sunday lunch-time.

He looked at me. I thought we'd see mum?

Doreen was in a home on the edge of the city. Every week we sat, one on either side of her, and watched while she dropped bright, frozen peas on the carpet. The peas ran under the wheels of her chair and got squashed into the matting. Sometimes I bent down and picked them up, trying not to get them in my nails, trying not to puke. I ignored the smells of bad food and old people's urine by looking out at the view of the car park and the grey blurriness of the hills.

He'd relate in detail what he'd seen on the box. Sitcoms and then the sport.

Doreen always stared straight ahead and said, Who is this man? Get him away from me.

I put on a sweet voice: It's your own son, Doreen. It's him.

What? What's the name of the woman he married?

Amy. That's me, Doreen.

Haven't they any children yet?

Not yet, no.

Well, bugger off then, the both of you.

We can go Sunday night, I told my husband and he made an impatient noise with his tongue. He didn't love his mother but he felt it was all down to him. His brother Darren was in Japan, OK for some.

Where are you going? he said.

Some pub with the girls, I don't know, it's not me organising it.

Lying came easily. I looked out of the window and pretended to watch a big yellow crane. His hand slid of its own accord on to my knee – that was because he was remembering the sex. Cheer up, I said, to get at him.

He said nothing. After a while, he slid the hand off and lit a cigarette.

He pulled up and I got out.

See ya, he went, already indicating to move away.

In the kitchen it was all go. Karen and Gwen were polishing up the glasses, going on about a film Karen had seen and Gwen wanted to see about a serial killer where the killer performed oral sex before using a butterfly knife on the victim. Jack was shouting at the new washing-up boy. And Hetty was working out the rota for next week, frowning at the paper pinned to the noticeboard, shaking her biro like crazy to make the ink flow free.

My foster world was creepy and electric. Plugs and sockets were a major feature. Brian liked gadgets. I'd sit listening to all those appliances humming. I'd drink my milk, avoiding the creamy lumps. I'd watch people being blown up in wars on TV.

At Christmas we had three different sized trees made of twinkly metal. A large green one for the lounge, a smaller silver one for the hall and a baby pink one for the kitchen. The base was heavy and the branches stuck into holes. You could cut yourself pushing them in. When the fairy lights were draped on, you flicked the switch. If it worked, fine. If not, you fiddled till it did.

A girl at school had been electrocuted drying her hair in the bath. A baby next door had died of liver failure and Eileen held coffee mornings for it. Old people died alone at Christmas, their bones stiffening in their chairs which were, you hoped, stuffed with fire retardant foam.

At Christmas it didn't matter that I was fostered. I got everything the others got.

Father Christmas in a red felt hat rode on the back of a white seagull. Tiny metal presents were in his sack. There were six of these altogether and we tried to spread them evenly over the tree.

28

There was no flesh between me and the Bishops. Eileen and Brian and Sally and then Freddy. Eileen did her best, but it was all papers and talk. What's flesh and blood? Not blood and string and fat like on a joint of meat, but just this person smiling and smiling at the stupidest things about you. Someone who took you for granted. I'd have given anything for that. I had this gasping worry I'd end up like Auntie, with no one to love but Jesus, folding and folding at the top of some back staircase.

I like you because you don't expect anything, my husband told me when we first got together.

Sometimes Sally and me put on Eileen's nylon slips and get married. We always marry Tom Jones. If you're Tom you stick your pelvis right out.

Sally and me are in bed together, practising for marriage – I don't know who's being Tom. The bed is hot and Sally's breath on my face is moist, her fingers fanny-smelling. Our nighties say: Keep Away From Fire.

Eileen sews us dog-type animals out of Jumbo cord. Sammy's my one, Dammy's Sally's.

Dammy isn't a name, I tell her and she says it is so I hit her.

Hitting won't solve things, says Eileen who is a Christian.

Sammy has orange buttons for eyes and this faintly berserk look I really go for. Dammy's small because Eileen started cutting him from a too-small cushion and ran out. OK, so Sammy's the superior animal, I know that, but secretly I love Dammy.

If we get a new thing, Eileen says, Let her get her fussy out of it first.

Sally always gets a bigger fussy than me. She is the pretty one, out-going and double-jointed, always doing the splits holding on to the see-through coffee table, front and sideways.

She wins ballet medals up to Elementary while I stay in Beginners. Eileen brings along soup in a thermos when she watches Sally – such dedication makes you famished. Sally has her hair up in a bun for exams and is allowed lacquer which stays in till the next wash. In bed I am so jealous of her hair, stiff with Elnett.

She collects glass animals and whimsies and her Swiss Cottage plays 'Hi Lily, Hi Lo', while my one just snaps open and shut. It seems a joke, that a couple as downright plain and awkward as the Bishops should come together and produce such a glamorous child.

I was getting on for seven when Sally was born and it was certainly bad luck for Eileen and Brian that after all those years they went and made a kid of their own just months after taking delivery of this stroppy six year-old who wet the bed still and screamed in church and got ringworm and headlice and spat lumps of Weetabix down the back of the radiator.

But you see it on TV: these couples sign the papers and just as soon as they do, sperm and egg come together and it makes you think somebody must be having a good old laugh Up There.

Being Christians they could never admit it but I reckon if Eileen and Brian could have taken me back right then, no questions asked, they would've. Or Brian certainly would've – exchange or refund. As it was, they kept me but their hearts stayed small and tight and furious.

I knew it was him straightaway by the silence.

Wednesday, after lunch, and I was mopping and chatting to the girls and sucking an ice cube from the end of my sneaked Bacardi. Karen rolled her eyes as she handed me the phone. Won't say who, she said.

Nothing. Silence. Then, Amy?

Who is this?

You're coming aren't you? On Sunday.

I told him I was, hadn't I said I would? I shifted the ice so it didn't make my teeth ache and swallowed the cold juices off it. I had a sore throat and my nails stung from pressing garlic.

Good, he said.

I was sick of the mystery. An idea occurred to me. Are you Justin Appleby? I asked him straight out.

No, he said and laughed but the laugh contained no surprise.

You knew him?

She left me for him.

Oh, I said, I'm sorry.

Don't be. I found her again.

Found her?

Why was I trembling? I steadied myself against the counter, wedged my hand under my arm so I wouldn't want to prise a chunk out with my teeth.

Yes, he said, I'm good at finding women.

You went all the way there to find her?

Not such a long way. Probably not as far as you think. One day I'll take you there – if you're good.

A taste like blood came into my mouth. Was she pleased, I asked him, That you found her?

He laughed again. Yes and no, he said.

What's that supposed to mean?

He hesitated. Maybe I'm too good at finding people.

What did you . . . ?

I'll see you Sunday, he said.

It was almost five when I left the restaurant, dark, the air fuzzy with a light rain. I had the key to Mara's place in my pocket and I considered stopping off at the

Garden, just a brief check, but decided against. My body felt flimsy and loose; I had to be alert if I was selling it.

I did the next best thing: stopped off at a cash machine and got a print-out of my statement. £2,600 in the black. And I'd only been at it six months or so.

He'd said he was good at finding people and I wondered again and again about how he'd found me. I'd come to this city in a haphazard way, so how come he had managed to be here too?

Brian eventually ran off with a Filipino cleaner from his church – a weeping, gesturing teenager who he'd got pregnant, the dumb fuck. And Eileen died of cancer just before their baby was born.

It was a boy. I wouldn't go near it or them. He wrote to me that Virgilia had to be cut open to get the baby out because being Filipino her hips were too small and you were supposed to feel in awe that he had found such a slender sex queen of a woman. But I hoped she had a massive scar which would make Brian go off her and that their union would burn in hell.

Straight after Eileen's funeral was when I left.

I got to Paddington with eight pounds-fifty and a tuna bap in my pocket and the departures board going chuck-chuck-chuck. I fancied a small town with trees and dogs and prams and old folk who're still married and the sun always out and drying the washing. I fancied cheese plants in the bathroom and a husband and a smooth white double bed with a clock radio by it.

I picked a place at random. The man said it was twelve-fifty one way, but I only had eight-fifty, so I said is there anywhere for eight-fifty? and he stared straight ahead and said, You must be joking, not unless you're under sixteen.

32

Eventually this old bloke came up. He had long yellow fingernails and an upset look in his eyes. He said would I have a drink with him at the stand-up bar over there and I thought how I'd far rather have a burger at the Burger King, starving as I was and with only the bap to last till God knows when.

So I said so.

How do I know I can trust you? he said.

Well you don't, I said softly, catching his eye as I spoke.

At the Burger King I ripped the ketchup sachet with my front teeth and he said I was a little bitch.

I didn't listen to him. I concentrated on the sweet onion sliding down my throat, the soft artificialness of the bread. You're a confident little Madam, he told me.

I laughed and touched his nylon thigh under the table. It cost me nothing and I could see he enjoyed it. He breathed a little harder and looked away.

Next door the pub was all fake lit-up and men slouched against the bright plastic ferns looking at their watches. I gripped the ten pound note he'd given me. I knew I'd have to pay on the train. Oh look at the time, I said, My train'll be off.

Tell you what, he said, but I was already sliding off the PVC high-up seat. He put out an arm to grab me, but too late. He shouted but I was running so fast over that marbly place, skidding past coats, thudding into sleeves and bags.

I had the greasy, screwed-up warmth of the note in my hand. With it I left the city.

One and a half years of being alone and then I met my husband.

The pizza kitchens where I worked were hot and dark and the boys played French cabaret tapes and

33

slept with each other, not me. There were piles of coats behind the door and mints by the till and the signs for the toilets were done in writing so snazzy and posh you could hardly read it.

In the city, tourists came for the waters and snapped themselves in front of the Roman baths where water poured from bright green holes and the air smelled of sulphur and nylon rucksacks and Kodak.

After I lost the pizza job I signed on for a bit and did nothing. It didn't matter, I was so in love with the city, the deep and fascinating calm of the place – the way didgeridoos were played by the shopping centre and there was always someone in a rainbow hat and people in wheelchairs sat limbless and smiling in the sunshine.

You could buy anything secondhand if you knew the right places because people died in their sleep and whole houses were emptied out and put on sale like intact, discarded lives.

You'd get paperbacks for ten pence and crumby cutlery and pins and plasticky things you wouldn't ever want. Silk blouses at the Antiques Emporium, and cracked dolls with sharp little teeth, heavy amber beads and flapping roses and rusty biscuit tins and falling-apart boxes with fraying leather fastenings.

A woman called Annette had a toy stall there – everything a hundred years old, wind-up monkeys and pin-head dollies and people made of tin with painted-on hair. Annette wore an appliquéd jumper in white and cream and these too-tight vinyl trousers which meant you saw the embarrassing outline of her pad when she was on.

She always had a plate of shepherd's pie or some-thing going cold from the café and her coffee cups were black inside 'cause you had to go to the Ladies to rinse them out and she couldn't be bothered. Annette let me work for her for a while, only I charged too little for things and after a while the dust was getting on my chest.

I traipsed around the market which smelled of mushy peas and I sat with my Diet Coke on the steps at the bottom of the bridge which had shops on like a little city and watched the ducks snaffling their beaks in the rubbish at the water's edge where it was brown and frothy with muck.

A child ran past with a red balloon, feet in new sandals like a made-up child in a book. The mother seemed satisfied and glad, her hair tied back neatly with a velvet clip. A man with a buggy was arguing with an overweight woman in Lycra cycling shorts.

I watched the river at its deepest point where it turned to glass, where it slowed and tricked you into thinking it had stopped just before it crashed over the weir.

Jack told me that rain fell on those hills ten thousand years ago, got heated at the earth's core, bubbled back up like a kettle boiling. Gallons of it still come up out of the ground every day, he said.

Ancient rain, I like that – like to think that's what we're living on: ten thousand years of hot water.

Hetty said she'd put me on the cloakroom and the upstairs bar to start with but that I'd wait tables on the busier shifts and some days I might even find myself washing up and how did I feel about that?

I'm not bothered, I said. I wasn't lying.

Great, she said, Let me tell you all about us. We've seven regulars actually, all really super people who've been with us since forever. Also a couple of older ladies who come in twice a week from Little Terton. It's a basic nine shifts a week but it's up to you if you want to do extra – we're always short, if you know what I mean.

All the while she clicked the button on her Biro in and out, occasionally diddling it against her teeth. You could tell she was efficient. She had on a short skirt which showed off her knowingly good legs and low-heeled ankle boots laced in a criss-cross. She spoke loudly and moved her elbows and pushed her fingers through her fringe. You could tell she was the outdoors type, grown up happy and well-off with plenty of brown bread and fresh air and laughing, slobbering dogs.

A bell rang then and she told me she had to go see to the flowers.

Well, we all muck in here, Sarah, she went.

Getting my name wrong, but I knew I had the job.

They took pity on me on the accommodation front, let me have a room upstairs. Five flights up and painted white and the ledge outside green with old pigeon shit. There was a bathroom – mostly my own – though once a week the seafood was delivered and the crayfish were dumped in the bath.

They shuffled and scratched with their long, whiskery legs, never keeping still, black stalky eyes feeling for the light. I managed to piss and clean my teeth without looking at them, but in the night I couldn't block out their sound – crawling up the sides of the bath again and again and falling back.

Jack said they had to go into the pot alive – a question of flavour and of ethics. He said it was more honest, to kill animals yourself if you were going to eat them.

Why is it more honest? I wanted to know, because when people like Jack and Hetty say they're being honest, it sometimes sounds to me more like they're just flaunting their opinions.

Think about it, he said.

There were two beds in the decent-sized room. I

slept in one and put my belongings on the other. I'd never had so much space in my life. I was drunk on the space and clean stillness of privacy. There was no curtain at the window and Hetty said she'd give me something to tack up, but she obviously forgot because she never did.

I undressed in the dark with only the stars spying down at me.

According to Jack, there used to be little black boy slaves in these buildings. But you'd never have known it, what with all the partitioning and paint jobs they'd done since and all the noise of them emptying out the pub and into the curry place down in Isabella Street.

Sometimes I sat there sucking at my fingers and watching the darkness settle on the city and it was eerie, like I was no longer in just this room but somewhere else as well. A bigger space. As if the room was cut up into these separate layers and I was only the top one and a thin and shivery one at that, like the brownish bit on one of Jack's salmon and ginger puff pastry pies.

The best thing about meeting and marrying my husband was getting out of that loneliness, plus a bathroom of my own without anything live stored in it.

Three

Sunday was a fresh, mild, unlikely sort of a day – the air soft, thick, mucky with the smell of rained-on leaves.

My husband told me to say hello to Paula for him. He liked Paula because her husband Derek had once bought a home office package off of him. I will, I said.

I was glad to get out. He was sitting there in T-shirt and pants reading the sports section and the whole place smelled of the skin of his face when he hadn't washed it for a couple of days, or else just rinsed and not used any soap. I knew he was pissed off with me by the way he kept shutting doors, switching off lights.

I fed Megan and shut her in, getting a thrill out of closing the door on her whiskery face.

Outside, everything was alive and lively. A band noise sounded like it was coming from Alexandra Park and the church bells had only just stopped – their echo was hanging in the air like a good smell.

Harris had said it was walking distance but on my map it looked quite a way. The actual road was almost on the crack. I did a lot of walking normally because my husband wouldn't trust me with his car, which was a company one, H reg. It was the same story as the makeup. He got me through my test but he didn't want me to drive because he knew I might get in and just keep driving and not come back.

I thought I'd set off briskly up Melly Hill and get on a bus if one came, but one didn't so I ended up standing in his road at ten past one, my face annoyingly flushed and sticky with sweat.

Stepping back into someone's drive, I checked myself in my compact and put on some powder. It was one of those roads where the houses are so big and far back you don't know if they're flats or not. Big low cars in dark colours which cost you. His place had black railings and a load of dark green, wet-smelling bushes and a dead bird lying on the steps up to the door where the empty milk bottles were.

There's a dead bird, I said as he answered the door, grinning at me like I don't know what.

Yes, he said, I've been meaning to move it, do come in.

He spent a long time just looking. Looking at me.

I let him, I didn't care. I even wondered if he fancied me. There was a massive red stain on his jacket, like wine and I couldn't get my eyes off it.

I'm sorry, he said, It's just – seeing you again after so many years – it, well, it moves me. Can you understand that? Do you mind it?

I looked at him and said nothing.

I don't want to embarrass you, he said.

I smiled. I couldn't think what else to do.

You don't know me, of course, he said, But I know you. Little Amy, he added softly as if to himself.

He came over and put his hands on either side of my face, his thumbs sweeping my cheek and looked at my eyes, nose, hair.

Little Amy, he said again and I felt my stomach heat up and fought an impulse to offer to suck his cock.

He released my face and poured me some wine and I used the space of him turning and fiddling with the glasses to get my breath back.

To you, he said and raised his glass with one eye

closed like he was measuring me. I took a sip and walked over to the window like they do in films. Everything I did was like I was watching myself from the outside.

Thanks, I said.

I held on to the glass tight with both my hands and looked around the big room all spattered with objects – a load of dark, expensive things on tables all covered in dust and bits of glass and pictures and books. I'd never seen so many books and I told him so.

Do you read?

I do like a good novel, a love story, but I wasn't admitting it among his fancy intellectual things. I shrugged.

Magazines, I said, But they don't count of course.

Everything counts, he said, like I could do no wrong – like everything I did was fascinating in his eyes.

OK, I was laughing now, I like to read.

We both laughed, him joining in with me and it felt friendly. He offered me a seat, and I sat.

I used to teach, he told me, Me and the rest of the world, but I'm too old now.

I thought he couldn't be that old. There was a young-ness in him, a springiness. He was white-haired, but his face looked too amused and sarcastic for an old man.

He poured more wine for himself though I'd hardly touched mine and pulled a photo from a drawer. Her: skirts blowing against her longish legs, light yellow hair flickering, cigarette cupped in her fingers and, coiled behind her ready to pounce, the sea.

I was surprised. I'd only a couple of snaps myself, saved for me by Eileen, and they weren't as good as this. You could see she was what you'd call fuckable.

He left me holding the picture. It had the triangle marks in the corners where it'd come out of a book.

Keep it if you want, he said.

41

Really?

She was your mum. And I've plenty more.

How come?

What? He looked at me.

How come you've photos of her?

Why not? he said quickly. She was my absolute love. We loved each other, your mum and I. Gary! he shouted at the door, Come and show yourself. Come and say hello to Amy.

So he lives here, does he? I asked, getting more confident now at questioning him.

Sure. He's my lodger, isn't he? My flatmate.

Gary came in. There was a rich whiff of cooking, but it didn't look like it came from him.

I've got to go out, he said. Sorry.

He had a beer in his hand but he hadn't even started it and he didn't bother looking over at me. I ignored him back. The picture was still in my hand and I saw how she was looking out at nothing, not at me, not at anything. A clean, sexy face without the burden of thoughts.

Gary pushed his fingers through his sticking-up hair.

Now? said Harris. You've got to go out right now before lunch. With Amy here?

I shan't be long.

I wondered if it was Gary's fat cheeks that made him look sulky or whether he would have looked sulky at any weight.

Bloody Christ, said Harris, but more to himself.

Gary took a rucksack off the floor and buckled it and went.

I sit on the sofa, Harris on a chair by the mantelpiece – a posh old fashioned one with legs that curve and velvet buttons all over. The sofa has springy hairs sticking out.

In the flat of my married life, everything's brand

new and modern and reasonable. Sharp edges, fixings, catches. We go to Sunday stores and pick up these Scandinavian pieces, wood-smooth and light as honey, flat-packed for self-assembly. You queue up with a ticket to collect them and they go in the back of the car.

At home my husband lays the pieces out carefully and then he makes them up. He never gets stuck. It takes him some time but that's the point. He looks so right when he does it, in his husband outfit of checked flannel shirt and jeans and big socks and a can open on the floor and he'll sip and frown as he reads the piece of paper back over to himself. Sometimes he complains about the quality of the finish or the stupidity of the instructions, but the final thing he'll be happy with.

And at the end of it all, we have more storage.

Harris looks at me like he can tell my thoughts, like he has special access to delve into my head.

What? he goes.

Nothing, I say, I didn't say a word.

I used to throw you high in the air, he says, Toss you up and catch you again. Are you telling me you don't remember that?

I shrug and smile. The sound of a radio creeps in from somewhere, I can't see where.

Do you have the whole house? I ask him.

He nods. But not the basement, that's a separate flat. I've been here nearly twenty years.

I left the island twenty years ago, I tell him, because I know it's true.

I know, he replies as if glad of the fact I'm tossing him, I know that.

Tell me everything about her, I say because the wine is making me brave and relaxed and unsteady.

43

He gives this sad little laugh. Everything? I don't know everything.

Tell me what you do know.

I take another big mouthful and look at his book-shelves so I won't have to look at his face. I don't know what sort of thing he's going to tell me, or how it's going to change anything, but it's what I've come for.

I sigh at the idea of all the talking we've got ahead of us. I want it and I don't, both at the same time, if that makes sense.

It's a long story, Amy, he says.

Yeah, I say. Go on.

I couldn't tell if his shyness was put on or not. He spoke quietly and he kept stopping, as if he was making it up, only you just knew he wasn't. Finally I put my feet up on his saggy sofa and lay back and gave in to the calm, slidey slope of his voice.

Pictures came out of the black, sparking in my head, flickering together and absorbing and replacing each other like TV as he spoke.

Some seemed truer than others and some bothered me because I might've made them up or not and anyway how would I know? Some I felt I'd realised all along but not let myself in on their secrets yet. And some were like when your head sinks into your pillow and all last night's perverted dreams come sliding in, askew and unasked for.

All I did was keep myself steady.

Maybe I sucked men off in my spare time, but I was scared of this, scared of what I might hear. The air seemed twitchy, but I kept myself firm and still. I kept my fingers on the stem of the glass of wine, the redness bobbing and rocking in the splashy sun.

Now and then I wondered whether all this was what

44

I'd hoped to hear – and I wondered what it was he planned to gain by telling me.

That he was her first lover I could well believe and I could also believe it when he said how cool and slick he'd been then – tall, dark and sulky, good with his brain as well as his hands.

He said he was a teacher on his first job at St Albans High School and he taught her English – books and essays and emotional discussion. You got points for showing parts of yourself. Maximum exposure. Jody had a way with her. She wasn't a swot but she was quick – jumping into ideas and then discarding them just as quickly. Quick to say things, quick to get involved. She offered up her heart for inspection and he liked that. He liked it a lot. Looked it over, made a point of forgetting to hand it back.

He sussed that she hung out with a crowd which included older guys (his own age) like Justin Appleby but as far as he knew she wasn't involved with Justin then. Some were doing the Art foundation course at the Poly and some were doing Law. They met at lunchtime at a café in town, fancied each other, bought the odd bit of grass. Police had busted the café once or twice and one kid had got expelled as a result, but it was the Sixties and younger and funkier teachers like himself tried to give space to the pupils. These kids were sixteen, seventeen. What business of theirs was it what they got up to, so long as they turned up to class on time?

She usually came in late, her jumper well-darned and a certain look in her eye. My mum. Her grey rucksack covered in ink scrawls, pink nail varnish clotting the snags of her tights.

Then one day he caught her crying in the lunch-hour next to the privet behind the science block. Are you OK? What the fuck does it look like? she said. My

45

flat's right by the school, he said. He added he was on his way there right that moment.

He made sure no one saw them enter the block.

She sat cross-legged on his big brown beanbag. He lit a joss stick, put on an LP. She asked if he always did this in the lunch-hour. He said it depended but, yes, he liked to unwind. Unwind. The word sounded dense and awful as soon as he'd used it.

Her patent shoes had platforms a little higher than the school allowed. When she lifted her hands to touch her mouth (a nervous habit) or make a point, the navy-blue triangle of her knickers was easily seen.

He said, Tell me about yourself.

She said she wanted to be a dental nurse.

What? And stare down other people's throats all day?

Someone has to do it, she said, I'm good with people.

I'm sure you are. But why not a regular nurse? Why not a doctor?

I don't like people dying.

They die in the dentist's chair.

Not often.

You're good at English language, at writing, he insisted. You should do something with that.

She said she didn't want to teach.

Teaching isn't the only thing, he said.

He decides not to move any closer. She's a bird that might fly at any moment. Lifting off from him, un-catchable.

So he tells her the story of his life, like people who want to fuck other people do. He tells her, a touch too proudly, how smack did in his brain. He tells her the tale of his breakdown and his brief career as a petty thief and then follows it with highlights from his in-carceration in a locked ward.

46

He sees the girl, suitably entranced.

He tells how he believed the trolleys in the Cash 'n' Carry had come to life and were after him, and how he fibbed to his (then) girlfriend and even – for Christ's sake – stole money from her. How he had lost twenty-four hours out of his memory, come to at a bus depot, hit a man for some reason and broken his jaw and came to be – God forbid – committed.

And there you have it, he tells this beautiful, listening girl whose limbs fold mathematically under her like something made of wood that you would pay a lot of money for, whose hair waterfalls over her shoulders. Smack, he says again, It's a brain fuck. Don't let anyone tell you different.

Why'd you do it? she asks, wistful, disappointed but swayed all the same by the glamour.

Sweetest thing in the world, he tells her. Better than sex.

Still she stares. Has he gone too far?

Look, he goes, What can I say? I'm over it now. Are you shocked because you thought I was one of them, a teacher?

She shrugs.

He thinks about moving in then, kissing her, but decides it's too soon, too close on the heels of his sad, zany life story. Instead, he puts in a bit of poetry about how the drug flies straight to your centre, like a heart-beat.

Gimme a break, she goes and he flushes, knowing he's coming over as a total prick.

She tells him he's a pretty good teacher – not what he most wants to hear. He says she'll be a terrific dental nurse.

She buttons her cardigan. He points out it's all done on the wrong buttonholes. It's how I like it, she says. Oh, he's old, old, old.

He walks her back to school and they make out they've met up in the park which borders the lower playgrounds. Marigolds winking at them from the beds.

Soon she's in his den every lunchtime, abandoning her friends at the café. At first she makes a show of bringing work with her but after a while her bag stays put in her locker.

What did you do? I want to know, All those times she came?

Well, we talked.

And – ?

Well . . .

I wait, squeeze my eyes so tight shut the air is black pricked with orange. I hear his breath, his pause, his deliberate lack of an answer.

She was quite something, your mother, with this fantastic smile and the blonde hair and everything. She was bright enough, like you.

I'm not bright, I say into the air.

Amy, love. Don't say that. You need to stop wasting your time, that's all.

How d'you know what I do with my time?

He says nothing. Sighs briefly.

How do you know? I ask him again.

Forget it, he says.

On with the story, I say.

She was a strong spirit, your mother, wayward too.

You just fancied her.

Have I denied it?

He told himself he didn't want her, but the thing about reading books all the time was they encouraged you to live out your fantasies, to pay attention to how you felt and feel things hard and then satisfy every fleck of an

48

idea, every whim. Love and desire and the hope of both. Apart from those, what else was there? Love and desire in the here and now. God was rubbish and life only existed to remind you death was waiting.

I laughed a bit and sat up slightly, asked him if I could smoke. He nodded. The wine had blurred my brain and the room had grown thick with emotions – his and, possibly, mine. I lit up and understood without seeing it that my hands were shaking.

I saw how he was sitting forward on his seat, running his hands through his too thin hair and picking away at the threads on his jacket as he spoke.

Yes, I liked her, she was risky. Risks brought me to life in those days.

Without risks you felt dead? I asked him.

Dead? No, not exactly – but numb. I felt numb.

You've had an easy life, I told him, All this time on your hands to get so interested in taking risks.

My father was a dentist, he replied, Made us rich by filling teeth that didn't need filling. I had the standard unhappy childhood.

You've had an easy life, I said again.

I felt him look at me. I was glad I had the window to look at and not his face. It was getting to me, all this telling. My mouth tasted sad and sour. My eyes hurt with thinking.

You don't trust anyone, he said, as if he'd just worked it out.

Who has there ever been to trust?

You could trust me.

There you go, I said, blowing smoke out, I knew you'd say that.

I laughed to myself, but he said nothing. Maybe I'd hurt him.

Go on with the story, I said, I feel we're just getting to the sex bit.

49

He coughed. I looked quickly at his face. It was all broken up, all clouded with pain.

She took all her clothes off to a Bob Dylan track.

School uniform: a skirt with little buttons at the side, polyester shirt with well-laundered inkstains on the cuffs. Her jumper smelled of sweat and school dinners and when she took it off, her hair lifted with the chill and static. She laid everything carefully on the chair. Her tights still held the squeezed-out shape of her feet and legs.

How old was she?

Fifteen, he says quickly. He knows that.

And you?

Don't know. Thirty-five, thirty-six, I suppose.

You do know.

Thirty-six, then.

We say nothing for a while. I lie there, sad and excited. I see how shrill and greenish the light is on the window because it needs a clean and because of all the bushes outside. All is quiet. Occasionally a car engine revs but nothing else.

I'm sorry, he says after a while, It's not what you want to hear, is it?

I shrug.

It was wrong, wasn't it? he says.

I stub out my cigarette. Wrong? Why? I say, If she wanted it too?

I can see now that it was wrong. We shouldn't have done it – I shouldn't have. You sound like an innocent, Amy –

I laugh and wonder what he knows. What's innocent about saying she wanted it? I ask him, And anyway why shouldn't I be innocent?

Come on, Amy, he goes, She was a baby, wasn't she?

We leave a slice of silence.

He waits. You don't want to hear about it, he says.

I'll hear anything. All these years, no one's been able to tell me anything.

Silence again. A hardness starts in my neck and trickles down.

What happened to you, when you left the island? he asks me.

I was fostered, I tell him.

Institutionalised, he remarks as if to himself.

Not a kids' home, I correct him, A real home.

He laughs at this. I'm sixty-six, he says. Do I seem that old to you?

I don't know, I reply, I don't know how old sixty-six is meant to seem.

I could have brought you up, he says, I brought Gary up. I could've brought you up, couldn't I?

I say nothing. He pours us both more wine.

I think: I'm going to be a bit more drunk now but so what?

I see the shape of my toes in my boots. I curl them and watch the little pockets of light as foot strains against leather.

We ought to eat, he says, Sod Gary. What are you thinking now?

I'm trying to imagine my mother.

She was fifteen, but free. Unafraid.

That's how you remember her?

She'd have done anything for me, you know. She loved me.

He said how they were having this big affair and then just like that, she went off with Justin, left school and disappeared. It rocked St Albans. Everyone said it wouldn't work out with Justin and that she would waste her life or get raped and murdered in a foreign country

51

when she could have finished her exams and gone to college.

All my fault. I made her wild, said Harris softly – and I noticed how he seemed quite stuck on the idea, the power of it, him and this young girl.

I'd expected to lose my job anyway, he said, So I chucked it in and went off to find her. I couldn't just leave her out there, not knowing where she was. Her parents were pretending it hadn't happened. Justin had pissed off. She was living in a shack on the beach with you, and already pregnant again when I found her.

Now I sat up, breath slipping and rushing round in my head. The room adjusted but not quickly enough.

No, I said, Not pregnant.

Oh yes, he said – and I knew he'd leaned forward off his chair and was touching my arm, his fingers on my shirt, though I couldn't really feel it, or at least maybe I felt it after I saw it – She was. Your little brother was born just a couple of months after I found her.

My brother? The taste of sick was in my mouth, making my voice curdle. I don't have a brother.

Paul, Harris said.

Paul? – the word flowered, almost familiar, in front of me. I didn't know what to do with it.

He was leaning towards me, not touching me but it felt like he was. My cheeks were hot. I couldn't tell from my drunken bones where one thing ended and another began.

I don't have a brother called Paul, I said.

But Amy, you did. For a while you did. I'm so sorry. I shouldn't be the one to tell you – I thought you knew, I really did.

I followed his shape with my eyes. What happened to him? I said.

Well, he died, love, he died. I truly don't know how or why. Little Paul. I can't believe you don't remember

52

– you used to carry him around, you were very good with him.

As he said these words, I remembered the hot heaviness of a baby in my arms and I knew he was telling the truth. There are things you put away, don't think about. Then they spring back. Cold lights crept up my spine.

Gary never came back but Harris's anger about him slowly dried up.

He seemed to brighten. He seemed pleased, or satisfied or something. He called me dear and love. He put on some classical music – sad, complicated music – then he went around putting on lights. The shades were covered in a fur of dust – it was a man's house all right. It was dark already, though it wasn't past three-thirty. I realised all over again just where I was.

When he went out of the room to cook, I followed him vaguely, like an animal. The kitchen window was dark, crammed with leaf.

That bloody fig, Harris remarked softly, Blocks out all the light – I know, don't tell me, I should prune it but I just can't bear to.

Books were everywhere – piled up on the kitchen floor, in cardboard boxes in the corridor. Mostly Gary's, Harris said, Due to go to the shop.

What shop? I asked him.

Secondhand books – I've a little business, nothing much, small premises. He runs it for me.

I wandered back in the big room and curled on the sofa and, as he cooked, I fell asleep. I woke a few minutes later to feel his big hands on my shoulders, propping me against the cushions. How I wanted to pull him down, give him a bit of pleasure, feel his tense and tempting weight on me.

You're exhausted, you've had a shock, he said – and the words sounded crazy and familiar.

53

He made me eat some pasta and some lettuce, holding the fork up to my mouth and babying me with sweet talk and offering me little sips of water in between.

I think I love you, I told him suddenly.

He laughed. No more wine for you, he said.

The pasta tasted good and I told him so.

You were hungry.

I'm always hungry.

The music was swerving around my brain, waking me up, making me miss the life I'd not had, the things I hadn't known till he told me.

I'm sorry, he said.

What?

About all this. I'm sorry. It's not how I imagined it, our speaking together.

What do you mean? It's not your fault.

I looked at his beautiful face, waited till the lines crept into focus.

I thought you'd know about Paul.

I was fostered, I said, shrugging. They never told me anything.

Maybe they never knew anything.

I have, I said, then stopped. I mean, I remember . . .

What, Amy? What do you remember? You look like someone who would remember –

There have been things in my head sometimes that I thought I'd made up –

What sort of things?

I don't know. My mother, stuff from the island. But I don't know if I really remember a baby.

You were in deep shock when you left, he said.

There was silence as we both thought about this.

I asked again how my brother died. What was it? Was he sick?

You must understand, Harris told me carefully, I

54

never spoke to Jody again after I left. I might have, but she died soon after Paul. It was terrible but I had to accept that she didn't want me. She'd made the life she wanted.

She should never have had kids, I said suddenly – and straightaway wondered why I'd said it.

Why do you say that?

I didn't answer. I was trying to see the roundness of a baby's face, the whiteness of an arm, a leg – trying to put it in the place where memory goes. Where memory is.

Harris sighed, touched my hand. You've blocked all this, he said, Haven't you? You've stashed it away – I don't blame you.

Did you love her? I asked him.

His face went quiet as he went over it in his head.

I thought about her all the time. She sucked up my life, destroyed my energy for anything else, any possibility of another person. I wanted her, head, heart and sex. I don't know, Amy, would you call that love?

We were quiet for a long time then, just giving it all some thought. I felt easy with him – easier than I'd felt with any one. Just me in the room was enough for him and I'd never had that with a person before. Maybe that's what family is – or proper love, which comes from the heart and doesn't bother with all the panting and squirming that's sex.

The afternoon was leaking away but I didn't care. My husband felt like somebody else's relative, our dog someone else's dog, waiting there together, padding around in that dark flat. Even the men in the Garden for the Blind were people I'd never known, things I'd done half-heartedly in a wicked dream, not bothering to experience them properly. I'll be different now, I thought.

I'd like to know more, I said. It's hard, knowing only so much.

I can understand that, he said, You were there, after all.

I was there, I repeated, hardly believing it.

Then Harris said that what he really wanted most in the world was for me and Gary to be friends.

Gary? I said, disappointed – for I'd forgotten Gary – Why Gary? Where is he?

Gary's lonely, he said. He's not always the way he was today. He was really quite rude and I'm hacked off with him.

I laughed. He's not a child, I said, I don't get it. He seems like more than a lodger. Is he some relation? Is he your son?

No, but he might as well be. Actually, I obtained him on the rebound from your mother. I went and fell for another pregnant woman. Fiona reminded me of Jody in lots of ways.

How? In what ways?

Lots of ways – he hesitated, smiled – Lots of ways, he said again.

And . . .?

Her boyfriend had walked out on her, scared. I was there at Gary's birth, holding her hand, and then in the months after, walking around with this poor crying fellow on my shoulder all night. Finally, when he was almost a year old, she left us both.

I stared at him and he laughed and shook his head again.

It's true, he said, But I – well – I didn't mind. I'd got used to him. I liked him – crying all the time and not sleeping much. I didn't fuss. I put the radio on, smoked a joint, waited for his mood to catch up with mine. It wasn't my fault or his, I hadn't made him. It didn't get to me on the inside like it got to her.

56

You brought him up? I said, Just like that? You never tried to give him back?

Actually, it's worse than that, he said. She came and took him when he was three, but she couldn't cope and returned him to me. He was very distressed. He went around peeing on the furniture for a while.

Silence, while I took this in.

Look, Harris said, We've only just met. You don't know me, I know that. It's all a big shock. But think about it. If you have any time for Gary, I'd love to see . . .

See what?

See how you get on.

I was silent.

What? he said.

I don't know. It's a funny thing to ask, that's all, I told him.

He shrugged.

What if he doesn't want to know me? I said, Why should he want to? Have you thought about that?

Gary's so inexperienced, Harris said, as if it was some correct answer he'd just thought up.

And me?

You're not.

I thought I sounded like an innocent?

Don't mess me around, Amy, he said – and I just stared at him, at a loss, not knowing what to do with it all.

Then suddenly it was later, the window black and I wasn't drunk any more and we were having tea and slabs of fruit cake he'd found in some tin, me picking out the sticky cherries and eating them first.

I've been here all day, I said.

Where the fuck is he? he said, meaning Gary.

Anyway, I said, I'm married. What about that? What about my husband?

57

I stared at the round, smooth holes full of crumb and air where the cherries had been.

I'm not asking you to sleep with Gary, he said, I can't see the problem.

I flushed. You don't know anything about me, I told him.

Amy, was all he said.

He sat back and stretched out his legs.

I reached out and put three fingers of my hand on his knee, where the material was shiny and worn. Then I touched his leg, the mannish hardness of the thigh. Then I stroked upwards.

He kept his face all unnoticing and said, What does your husband do?

Sells computer stuff, software. I laughed.

That's not funny, he said.

You're right, I said, It's not.

He picked up my hand and put it back on my own knee. I looked at it.

Gary's a good boy, he said.

I believe you.

Maybe your husband and Gary would get on, he said, I mean as Gary sells things too – second-hand books with mouldy spines and the covers falling off. He's crazy about them. You might have seen my shop – do you know the little road just off the bridge next to the estate agent's?

I shook my head. I don't think they'd get on, I said.

In fact, come to think of it, said Harris, as if he only just had, The shop's right next to the Garden for the Blind.

He began to laugh.

Time passed – at least two days – and now I had a new life, a new self, as it were, through Harris's eyes. I badly wanted to see him again, but I knew better than to phone. Friendships aren't made that easily; people turn chilly on you. I've never risked pushing myself at anyone and being turned down.

He wasn't a young man, but I was thinking about him all the time – crazy, loving thoughts and sometimes sexual ones too. I can't deny it – I'd have been glad to make him happy in that way.

Blocking this madness out didn't help. In one day my life had turned itself over. So what was it? Was it love? Jesus, he's just some old guy, I told myself – a guy with a total need to talk. Is talking so attractive? Yes, blared out this voice within me, Talking's what you haven't had, Amy, these long, sad years.

I thought about it so hard and grew so sick over it that I couldn't tell who was the barmiest, him or me.

That afternoon turned to pure gold in my head. I kept on living it but with extras – thinking up new, better replies to things he'd said, questions I never asked and meant to, things I'd never told him and should have. Mentally I went over that room till I knew it by heart, looking for clues. The one that kept coming up was Gary.

He'd said we would be friends, that was definite, but what in fuck's name did Gary have to do with it?

Two days and I smoked, walked in the Garden for the Blind, and sat on my bench as usual, but I worried that I was being watched. By him or by Gary. I looked around nervously, like someone in a film. How was I to know? But it was all normal, the paths empty except for a bloke or two, the leaves light yellow and shaking, the traffic sending its blue fumes from the steep road into town.

I looked around me and then I worried that I wasn't being watched. He'd made out that I was a mystery to him, something worth taking notice of, but would he ever call me again? Was that it – a shared afternoon and a phone number you never dared ring? Both ideas bothered me.

I sat in the Garden and when a man approached, I tossed my plait that I'd lived in for two days and two nights and gave him a look till he couldn't take it any more and looked away, then I moved on. Nothing else. I heard some words spoken after my disappearing shape and maybe they were about sex, but I wasn't paying any attention. The path was damp and gritty, puddles with leaves and stuff floating in, green tips of daffs poking through the freshly turned soil.

The edges of my hair smelled of wool, skin, smoke. I picked up the tail in its laggy band and sniffed it for comfort.

A gardener in brown clothes was trailing up and down the paths and far-away, someone was having a bonfire. I despised the bird noise and the wetness. I noticed how downtrodden my old shoes were and made a note to buy a new pair. I thought of how I must look, with my sore lips and tired eyes and hands wandering all over the place.

And anyway, where were the blind? I'd never seen a blind person in the Garden, which was meant to be for them. Not even in summer when you nearly drowned in the amazing smell of all those plants growing.

Eleven o'clock on the third day, he phones. I've done laying up and have moved on to the cold table with Karen, both our coffees going cold on the side.

I grab the phone.

Amy –

Yes?

His voice and mine hold on to each other; it's sweet.

How are you? he goes.

Fine. I'm fine.

Gary would really love to see you.

Gary? I suck pesto off my thumb. Gwen indicates that she's doing crusts of new bread out of the oven with Marmite on and do I want one? I make a thumb up sign that I do.

See me? (What a laugh – this fat bloke would surely do anything rather than see me?)

But he sounds serious, setting me up with this man.

Well, how about a drink? he says in that posh voice of his.

With you?

No love, with him. (I hear him smiling, ache to see it.)

If that's all that's on offer, I say, Tell me when.

Name an evening?

It would have to be afternoon. I get off at three.

OK, he says. Tomorrow. Why don't you turn up at his shop? I'll tell him to expect you.

Gwen passes me the bread and I hold it between finger and thumb.

Jesus, I go, suddenly pissed off.

What? he says.

All these instructions –

Please, he says in a softer voice, Do it for me.

Tell me where the shop is, I say.

I'd met my husband through a friend who'd lured me on a last-ditch blind date. We were well-matched, each with our batches of disappointments in tow and nothing else going on. He told me I was sweet. I was moved that he had managed to get me so completely wrong.

We didn't marry in church because we don't believe in hypocrisy and I didn't wear white, it's too draining. The registry office was followed by a bit of a reception in the community hall at the end of his aunt's road.

Finger food and bubbly and a cake with us standing

61

on top – him and me looking out at the view of the rest of our lives. It made me dizzy to think of it, all that time rushing past our feet, the whiteness of the sugar stinging your eyes. We cut it together, both our hands on the knife and there was a photo taken of that and it went straight in a frame on the TV. In it, I'm laughing and my teeth look nice and strong, but he is already an echo of his future fed-up self.

His mum came out of the home for the day, though it was before she went downhill and she was better in company then – happy just to sit in the corner and smile from her chair and chew, swallow, listen, get taken to the lav once or twice.

Soon there were horseshoes and hearts in everyone's hair, pink, yellow and silver – shiny party colours. His aunt went round with a black bin bag, picking bits off people.

Look at this radiant creature, she kept on going every time she looked at me and I knew I was looking good in a pink slub silk suit nipped in just enough at the waist, with navy courts and a little navy hat with a bit of a veil.

I'd chosen the pink so the suit could be used for some other occasion at a later date but of course I never put it on again. Clothes get contaminated, so it went to the dry cleaners and stayed in its polythene. What a waste.

At six the lights went off and the disco came on.

Love you, he said and kissed me on the outside of my mouth and then, later, as Ultravox and Pet Shop Boys played and they turned some more lights off, he went further in with his tongue.

Four

You have to be careful your teeth don't scrape on the thin skin and to be honest it helps that mine aren't exactly straight. An overbite. My mouth is on the small side, so oral amounts to a workout for my jaw. He is trembling, whites of his eyes lighting up his pale ginger face, as I feed his hardish, blue-tinged cock into my mouth.

The more I flick my tongue around, the quicker they come, the less my face aches, so I'm usually happy to get right on with it. But this time he puts his hand on my head, grasps my hair till my scalp hurts.

Not so fucking fast, he growls in that voice thickened by little grains of desire. His pubic hair brushes my bottom lip, smells of toilet. The gingery hairs on his arms are standing up like an army. Only his belly's white and free of hair and freckle.

I slow down. It is a fact that you don't cross a man with a hard-on. I close my eyes. He keeps his hand on my head but gentler now, thumb rubbing my hairline in rhythm with the push of him, reminding me of dogs and stroking.

By the time he comes, I've tried to think about my bank balance, but instead got snatches of the island – me pulling my two feet through the hot, white sand, carrying my brother high above my head, my shoulders, his baby laughter exploding in my heart. As he ejaculates, as I lose the day-dream, my arms are tight with loss and shock. His semen pulses into the

63

minty rubber – feels like the loss of blood, a jolting spurt, unstoppable.

I can't tell if my head or my heart is hurting most. I come up for air, dry crying, because the tears are all burnt up.

I don't want to do this, said Gary, his big body unruly and startling, the way it filled the doorway of Blecker's Bargain Books, And neither do you. Go home, Amy. You needn't worry. I'll tell him we saw each other.

You'll lie?

He shrugged. It's not a lie. We did see each other.

OK, I said. I agreed with him but I was torn. The idea of him happily fibbing to Harris bothered me. And I didn't want to spend time with him either, but I didn't completely want to go.

This is his shop? I said, for conversation.

He nodded, but he didn't smile and he kept his big long arm over the doorway.

His shop.

You like it? I asked him. He made a face which said it was OK.

Just books?

I looked at his straight, sticky-up brown hair, his fat face with the fallen angel look. There was something exotic in his fat face – something hard to discover. He didn't often look you in the eye but when he did, you noticed.

Just books, he said and the way he said it was kind of definite, like he was an actor or something.

The way you speak, I said –

What? he said.

I don't know. It's funny.

He smiled, but not much.

On the window it said BOOKS BOUGHT AND SOLD and the woodwork was roughly painted in bottle green, but it needed another coat. There was a box outside with paperbacks in and a handwritten sign said, *Everything in here 20p.* And an arrow pointing down. The books were faded and curly, like they'd been out in spotting rain.

Maybe it was because Gary wasn't interested in me that I didn't want to go.

I pretended to look at the books, then I said goodbye. The bell dinged as he went back in, but he caught it with his hand and stopped the noise.

I walked slowly back across the bridge and bought some chocolate from the newsagents and sat on the bench outside the Yamaha showroom in the bright sun and unwrapped a piece. It broke softly on my teeth and the creamy sweetness leaked on my tongue and mixed with my spit. I didn't know what I was thinking. I felt there was something big and hefty to consider and no clear space in my head for anything else.

It was one of those days with a blue sky but chilly if you took your coat off.

I felt sick and wished I hadn't eaten the chocolate.

I didn't want to go home.

My husband said he'd almost met his target that week and it was only Wednesday.

God, I said, That's great.

It can't have been the right answer, because he gave out a big sigh like he'd been building to something and the moment was now. The room was dark and hot, the news on – men walking and talking against a blue background. My husband plunked down his coffee mug, shoved his hands in the hard, greasy fur at Megan's neck and looked at me.

I'm going to ask you something straight, he said, And you're going to answer it straight – a simple yes or no.

I looked at him, waited – for it wasn't up to me – folded my arms.

Are you seeing someone else? he said.

I was so calm I wanted to laugh. I said, That's what you think is it?

All these times you stay out – I'm not stupid – I know your shifts.

I swallowed. You know my shifts, I said – and knew it was true, he did.

Just answer my question.

I knew my husband, too, the way he wouldn't budge over some things. He'd collected his anger and made up his mind and he was going to be – well, the frown was embedding between his eyes.

I said, There's no one.

Pardon me for asking, he said, But it's what you think when your wife doesn't bother coming home.

I don't know what you're talking about, I said, but he butted in quick with, Where did you go on Sunday?

You know where I went –

Don't say Paula, he said, I know it wasn't Paula. You need a new story, Amy.

I sat down, felt for a cushion, took it on to my lap and played with its springy softness.

I saw a man – I told him, and I watched his face, watched the sign that his insides were freezing up with the knowledge. I wanted to give him a scare, why not? Who knew my mother, I added.

He looked at me – eyes screwed up into hard ridges of flesh with slices of liquid in them. What, he said, Who?

A man of sixty-six. An ex of hers. We talked.

What's his age got to do with it? said my husband.

I laughed.

I don't get it, he said. What man? How do you know him?

He knew her on the island, I explained calmly.

66

He's Greek?

I realised the thought hadn't occurred to me. No, I said, I don't think so. Not even slightly.

My husband bit his lip. He hated me doing things without him. Now, I knew just what he'd do next: try to cast doubt.

How do you know he's telling the truth? he said, This man? Where did you see him?

I explained to him how Harris had come into the restaurant and that he didn't live far away.

You went to his home?

I nodded.

Here, in this city? What road?

I told him – my husband had the whole city mapped out in his head and knew Melly Hill quite well, as he had a couple of clients there. I watched him, struggling with the facts which I'd by now got used to.

What proof have you got? he demanded.

What do you mean, proof?

Of what he says – that it's true?

I shrugged. He showed me a photograph of her.

My husband snorted. A photo! He could've got it anywhere, think about it. You think it's safe, just to go to someone's home like that?

I smiled.

He just happens to live here, so close to where you've ended up –?

Plenty of people live here, I said, and then I added, I know. I know it's not normal, but extraordinary things happen and one happened to me. That's why I didn't tell you. I knew you'd say oh yeah, Amy –

You never tell me anything, he went.

I want to tell you things, I said, wondering if it was true.

We don't share anything anymore, he said, You and me –

I felt tears coming to my eyes which was handy. I want to share, I said – and this time it was definitely a lie but it came easily.

Baby, he said, in his old voice – and I smiled and a fancy, girly tear ran down.

He put his hand out and I took it and then immediately let go, 'cause I knew I was coming on and didn't fancy sex.

He gripped my knee. I'm sorry, he said.

I'm sorry too, I said and I numbed over and let him kiss me.

Saturday morning, Harris called in at the restaurant.

He put his head in through the back kitchen door which opened out directly on to the street. Colin gave me a shout and I saw Hetty look up to see who it was asking for me at that time of day.

A bad moment?

No, I said, going so red it wasn't true.

How are you?

I'm fine.

He had on a tweed coat and his cheeks looked dry and pink under the grey stubble. I had a knife in my hand from skinning the tomatoes and we both looked at it a moment so as not to look at each other.

You saw Gary, he said. It wasn't a question.

The hotness of my cheeks wasn't dying down.

So that's nice, he said, How was it?

How do you mean? I asked him.

With Gary? How did you get on?

I put my knife down on the orange beer crates by the door and wiped my fingers on my apron. I hadn't any lipstick on and hated to feel my pale, ragged lips.

What did he say? I asked him carefully.

He never tells me a thing, said Harris.

Fine, I said, It was fine.

You need to take the initiative with him, you know, Harris said, He's shy. He won't do anything. He has no confidence. It's all tied up with his weight. Well, that's my theory.

You're full of theories, I said.

He smiled.

He's very . . . I began.

Very what?

Very – I was trying around in my head for the words but none came.

Convincing, said Harris, He's very convincing.

I said nothing. It hadn't been what I was going to say. He was a man you couldn't argue with. A delivery van had pulled up and a man came in behind him with a box of shallots. Harris moved out of the way.

I do wish you weren't married, he said suddenly.

What's that supposed to mean? I said.

Gary needs a girlfriend, he laughed, as if it was an OK thing to say.

I stared. You're incredible, I said. And anyway, why would he be interested in me? You can't just make people do things –

Harris looked sharply at me for a moment. You're right of course, he said, but I felt like he was just shutting me up. But I know Gary, he added, and he touched me – one finger on my kitchen-cold face. Drop by tomorrow, he said. Why don't you? We're around, I'm sure.

Oh, I'm afraid I'm busy tomorrow, I said.

But the next day I left my husband glued to the sport and said I was off out for a walk and I found myself, sure enough, heading up Melly Hill with Megan fussing at my side – in one of her annoying moods where she has to check every smell twice. There was a rough wind and the clouds were moving in one solid block of grey, the pavements turning to ice under my feet.

I walked as fast as I could, ignoring Megan going back to every gate post, ignoring the kiddies shrieking and riding bikes over slippery paving. Dusk was down on everything when I reached their house, the light draining away. I called to Megs and put her on the lead and tugged hard on it to show her. I can't stay long, I'd tell them, Got to get the dog back.

But their house was dark, no sign of life. I went quickly up the steps and pressed the bell. The dead bird had gone and there was a black plastic rubbish sack by the dustbin, which Megan sniffed. A wodge of circulars was shoved in the door, three empty milk bottles next to the mat.

I pressed the bell again. No reply.

The windows had a yellowish emptiness, as if no one lived there.

I walked home feeling fed-up, like a kid whose sweets are taken away. I made Megan stay on the lead and every time she tried to linger I jerked her along. Outside our flat, a street light kept coming on, then going out again as if it couldn't make up its mind.

Inside, he was snoring and there was slalom skiing on the box. Megan sidled over to him and sniffed his legs as if they could provide a clue.

I didn't used to want a child – couldn't see the point of making someone else who was going to rely on you and break your heart then criticise you when it all went wrong.

And Freddy was the only baby I ever knew, and I hated him. The first sign of him on his way was when Eileen threw up on my school spellings and though the book was covered in Fablon, there was always that faint, sweetish whiff of sick.

Freddy was pulled out of Eileen using salad servers. I thought of the sharp, cold, metal fork and spoon rooting around in her fanny and it made me go hot inside. Freddy's head was dented and covered in fuzz which brought mildew to mind, and his skin was yellow like an old smoker's thumbs. He cried all the time. He was an easy person to hate.

Then Eileen got hormone trouble and chucked a gravy boat at Brian and Bisto got in the controls of the TV and you could never get ITV with a clear reception again.

There was a girl at school who carried a small flick-knife in her rucksack. Her mum had swallowed cleaning fluid on the quiet and died. It was depression due to hormone trouble. I was so scared Eileen would go the same way and then I'd be put in care.

Sometimes Brian took the baby out in the car and drove round and round the block and then crept back into the hall with this petrified look on his face. It made you laugh, this great big man shitting himself and that shrimp of a baby calling the shots. Fred would be fast asleep, but then those pig eyes would snap open as the carrycot touched the carpet and it would begin all over again.

I wasn't surprised when Brian ran off with the young, firm-fleshed Filipino, but I was gobsmacked he planted another kid inside her. You'd think they'd learn. All that crying and creeping around all over again. You wouldn't wish it on your worst enemy.

Monday, the restaurant was closed as usual, so we all met up in town for a drink: Stuart and Paula and Gwen and Karen, Mervyn, me and Colin the other second chef.

After a quick half in Landers, Stuart said why not all pile into the two cars (Paula's Honda and Stuart's rusty 2CV) and drive out to Cold Wenton where it was much nicer?

I'm not fussed, I said, because a pub was a pub as far as I was concerned and they didn't get any cheaper out of town, Only I'm not getting in the same car as that asshole Mervyn.

For God's sake, he went, but I wasn't going anywhere with him breathing on me, so I got in with Stuart and Gwen.

It was a fifteen-minute drive – dark and lightly pissing with rain. As we drove, Stuart brought up that he'd been to see Auntie's grave.

How was it? Gwen asked him, her voice all quiet and respectful.

Well it was all right, actually, he said, this put-on brightness that made you sick entering his voice. There was this good feeling – a sense of calm, if you know what I mean.

I told him to cut out the sense of calm crap, but he kept on smiling in his maddening Christian way and I watched the up and down of his family-size Adam's apple which you could pick out in the flicks and flecks of light from passing cars. It was covered in small, short hairs. I wondered how he shaved without nicking it.

Amy, I know what you think, but I promise you, she's at peace.

What's funny? Gwen asked me, because I couldn't help it, I was cracking up.

A grave is a hole in the ground, I said, A body's a body. What's so fucking peaceful about it? I don't know anyone dead who wouldn't prefer to be alive.

There was a patch of silence then and I could tell they thought me a sad fucker, with no romantic notions of death, no communing with God and calmness and that.

In front of us a stoat-type creature was creeping

72

across the road, eyes glancing greenly in the headlights. Look out! said Gwen and Stuart slowed, peering forward over the wheel like in a bad movie.

But you don't know, Stuart said at last, being so generous and understanding, How the dead feel, do you?

I laughed.

They feel nothing, I said. What's wrong with nothing?

The stoat's eyes had left a prick of light behind, fading to red. I yawned so hard my jaw clicked. We got out. The air was bitter and punchy with woodsmoke which caught at the back of your throat and made your eyes go wet.

The pub table was sticky so I put my purse on the seat next to my bum. I wished I hadn't come, wished I'd made them all stay in town, then I could've sloped off early.

What's up? said Mervyn, meaning to get on the right side of me. He thought he was so great – he was the type to read men's magazines and leave them sticking out of his black nylon bag in the back room at work.

When he put a hand on my shoulder, my skin fizzed with hatred and I told him to fuck off.

All the fucking I ever get to do, he said.

Stuart's car keys with a rubber fried egg were on the table and I picked them up and felt them, then put them down and rolled and unrolled the red and black towelling mat.

Colin said something inane, then burped and apologised.

Karen put down my vodka tonic.

I thanked her and watched her stuff notes back in her money belt.

I folded the mat four times and tried a fifth but it wouldn't go. Brian once taught me that there's a fixed number of times you can fold anything, whatever its size. He did it with the napkin in a Chinese and then later with my gummed origami paper and sure enough it worked out the same.

Paula was telling Karen about the four-star hotel in Kiddenton where she and her husband were going for their anniversary. You get champagne and flowers and a jacuzzi in the room, she said.

I laughed at the idea of her and hubbie in a jacuzzi together.

What? she said.

Oh, nothing, I went, though I was sick to death of hearing about her life – of how she was married to a fireman and was a member of Mensa and how that morning her dogs had got in the bathroom and eaten up her contraceptive pills.

Gwen and Stuart were on about this programme on TV that said what time of day you were born affected your whole personality.

Come on, Amy, what time were you born?

I said I didn't believe in that crap, but they only laughed and said I must tell them or they'd have to guess. I stood up.

I can't, I said. Sorry.

I was laughing, but the room was going far away from me, the edges of people bleeding off into one another like an out-of-focus photo. Everyone was dressed in brown, or that was how it looked to me.

Just off to the ladies, I said quietly.

Need a hand? Mervyn brushed my bum with his fingers.

Get off, I said.

As I moved towards the door with the female silhouette on it, I saw a youngish fat man sitting in a corner by the bar alone. It was Gary. He saw me instantly and nodded at me to come over.

I didn't know what to say. He said, Hiya.

He moved up, all calm and unsurprised. He had on a kind of beige linen-type jacket much too thin for the cold weather and a woollen scarf and next to him was a pink plastic bag. His face was hard to read in the dim, pub light.

I sat down and he said something I didn't catch. He said it again.

A drink? Can I get you one?

I've got one, I said, and looked over my shoulder. Over there.

He followed my eyes. He must have seen Paula and Gwen and co, but he didn't show it in his face.

But I don't want to go back over there, I admitted, realising it.

He smiled – the first time he smiled at me – and it was a nice thing to see, his face jumping out at me in full, de luxe colour.

He bought me another vodka tonic – ice, no lemon. It sat on the bar mat with its shovelly meltings of ice. There was someone else's lipstick on the glass's rim, so I turned it and drank from the other side.

Dirty glass? he said in a concerned way.

I'm not fussed.

I've got my car, he said, I can give you a lift back into town if you want.

I thanked him. You're all alone?

He pretended to look around him. Oh gosh, he said, Yes I am – and I laughed a bit because he was trying to be nice.

I don't know you, I said then.

He frowned.

I don't want to . . .

What? He looked at me.

I mean, you don't have to sit with me just because . . .

Please, he said, and shifted his eyes to the floor with its pattern of stickiness and rubber sole marks. Please sit with me.

Where's Harris? I asked him, for something to say.

He shrugged and moved his eyebrows up, like I should see it was none of his business.

We sat in silence a bit after that, but I didn't mind. Someone had put music on and I settled gladly back in my seat, not even bothering now to look over at the others.

What's in the bag? I said, meaning the pink one and he smiled and passed it over. It felt light, soft, squashy.

I put my hand in, pulled out what looked like a tiny towel in pale striped colours. He watched my face.

Baby clothes?

He took them from my fingers and laid them flat on his huge knee. There were three vests with poppers, an all-in-one thing and a hat with earflaps.

I asked if he had a baby.

No, he smiled, They're for my sister's kid.

You went out and chose these?

He nodded.

God, I said, My husband would never do that.

I didn't know you had a husband, he said quickly.

Didn't you? I said, surprised.

No.

I didn't know you had a sister.

He smiled. People do.

Where does she live? I asked him.

Oh, a long way away, he said. Another country.

Where?

I'll tell you some other time?

Why the mystery?

76

There's no mystery. It's not interesting for now. I'll tell you one day.

I looked at the clothes on his lap.

Will they fit? I said.

Maybe not, he said, By the time they get there.

One by one he put them back in the bag.

What's the baby's name? I asked him and he seemed to have to think about it.

Ellen, he said and I told him it was nice.

How can you have a sister? I asked, and he obviously didn't understand, so I told him what Harris had said, about bringing him up from a small baby.

His face went closed and he put down his drink, but he said nothing.

What? I said.

He started to speak and then seemed to stop himself. Then he said, Look Amy, forget it. I'm not being funny or anything. Just better not tell Harris we had this chat.

What do you mean? I said, Isn't it true, what he told me?

When he tells you something, just don't question it. Say nothing. It doesn't matter.

But . . .

He has helped me, Gary said, In lots of ways.

But he's a liar?

He's a good man. I can't say any more.

I laughed angrily because all the mystery suddenly seemed stupid to me. Just tell me, I said, Why he's told me a lie?

It's not a lie, Gary said.

Why would he lie to me? I said, ignoring him. He'd know we'd talk. He wanted us to see each other. If we saw each other, then you'd tell me the truth.

Yes, said Gary, You're right. Let's leave it at that, OK?

He said it like he'd closed off from the subject, stopped caring.

I still don't get it, I said.

Don't try to. You won't. I told you, it doesn't matter.

All around us, the pub was full of people laughing, but I felt terrible, emptied out. I had more questions.

Why did you leave, the other day?

Gary picked up his keys.

You'll despise me if I tell you, he said.

I don't despise people.

OK. I was scared, he said.

Scared?

Of you.

I stared at him.

You see? he said. Come on – he put down his glass and touched my arm. Time to go.

His car – I don't know what make – was one of those falling-apart old ones you see in the street with dents in and a For Sale sign and an optimistic figure after it.

On its last legs, Gary said as he had several tries at shutting the door.

Can't you get a new one? I asked him. I was used to men like my husband, who cared about cars.

Why would I want to? he said. This one goes.

The belts didn't plug in either and the mesh at the front didn't close when you turned the knobs, so the weather came in all over us. In the back was a blanket covered in hairs.

Have you got a dog? I asked him, because I loved all dogs except Megan.

No, he said. A friend's collie sometimes rides in here. I used to have a dog. I'd like another.

I asked him what breed it was and he said, Oh, nothing really. Just a mix of this and that.

Then he asked if I had one and I said about Megan, but not rubbing it in too much about hating her. I said how I'd like to breed best of all – go in for it seriously and all that.

Funny, he said, Me too – and I really liked him for saying that, even if it wasn't especially true.

We drove in silence. I was still going over what he'd told me. I was also nervous, wondering if Harris was right, that Gary had seen me doing business in the Garden for the Blind. The idea bothered me quite a lot. I thought about all the times I'd tried to make sense of things and it had been my fault. This time it wasn't, but knowing that didn't help.

After a mile or two he turned the noise of the heater down and in the quiet, he said, Tell me about yourself, Amy.

Harris knows everything, I said, He knows more than me.

I'd rather hear it from you.

What part would you like to hear?

Whatever you'd like to tell.

That makes it hard, I said – and then, before I could think, I heard my voice saying how I was born on the island of Eknos –

Eknos? he said.

In the Med somewhere.

Ah, he went.

You know where that is?

Roughly.

I don't, I said, adding for I don't know what reason, Harris does.

Look, I have huge respect and all that for Harris, Gary said suddenly, But we're not close in the way you seem to think.

Why're you saying that? I asked him. What do I think?

I don't know, he said, I don't know what you think. I just thought it needed saying.

I thought about this. It had needed saying. Harris and Gary were now separating before my eyes, peeling apart and turning into different people – two sticks of men, one fat, one thin. I smiled to myself and watched the twisty darkness of the road, a little wetness spraying up here and there.

I was born at four in the morning, I said, surprised again at how easily the words trickled out, The time when most people die.

You find that significant? he asked me quickly.

What?

That you were born then?

I laughed and he laughed too. He took cigarettes out of his pocket and bit one out of the packet with his mouth and offered me one. I shook my head and then wondered why I'd refused when I was feeling so nervy.

Actually a nurse told me that, I said. Why do they die then? Have you any idea?

Probably metabolic, he said and I realised he'd been keeping his cleverness from me, as kind people do.

Harris told me I had a little brother who died, I said.

He told you? You didn't know?

I'm not sure, I said, wondering. It's really hard to say. A part of me seemed to know and another part didn't. Why? D'you think that was a lie, too?

Gary seemed to think about this. What do you think? he asked me.

I don't think it was, I said. It was like someone telling me something I knew all along. But – what – are you saying it was – a lie?

No, he said.

But it could be? I insisted.

He paused again. No, he said, I don't think so.

80

We were silent, black rain on the windows.

He seems – Gary began.

What?

Well, so crazy about you – so delighted to have come across you again. He's moved by you, isn't he?

How d'you mean, moved? I asked him.

He's a funny man, was all Gary would say.

He says he loved my mother, I said.

Yes, said Gary.

I looked at the side of his fat face, washed blue by the light, traces of stubble on the bigness of his cheeks. We were heading along the dark lane which would join the main dual carriageway back into town. Gary peered at the road. On either side of us, faraway white lights.

Please forget what I told you tonight, he said suddenly, I mean in the pub –

You didn't tell me anything, I said.

OK, forget what I implied.

I said nothing.

We were quiet for a while, just the rattle of the car and the buzz of the night. Then suddenly he pulled in and stopped. He shut off the engine and the lights and I saw the shiny, pale wideness of the moon rolling by for a second before it burrowed into cloud.

We were nowhere. It was a gate with a mud track in front, just off the lane. No cars around, nothing. I thought the thin shapes bending in the black air were probably trees.

What is it? I asked him, as he sat there, hands on the wheel, staring straight ahead.

He sucked in the last of his cigarette, crunched it in the ashtray which was full to spilling.

Amy, he said, not looking at me, staring straight ahead. A little tic zig-zagged over his eyelid and it was like seeing into his body for a split second.

What?

81

I suddenly thought –

What? I said.

I suddenly wondered how it would feel, to have you lying on top of me.

We were still, the words the only moving things. I did my best to take in this new situation. Of all the men I'd come across, not one had ever said a thing like that.

You wondered how it would feel? I said, half-laughing and half-afraid.

He sighed, laid his forehead on his hands which were still on the wheel.

You're sending me up? I said, seeing it, but not minding.

He didn't move. No, he said simply.

I asked him for a cigarette and he passed me one without looking up – and his lighter which was a light plastic type in pink. I breathed it in and felt my body thank me.

You're saying you want sex? I said and laughed, though inside I was disappointed.

He shivered. I don't know what I'm saying, he said.

I felt sorry for him suddenly. He was nice enough. I could see him breeding dogs out in the country – and I respected that he'd been almost honest with me about Harris.

It's OK, I said. It's cool. You can say whatever you want to me, I'm not shocked.

It's not a question of what I want.

You want to talk about your cock?

He shook his head, then smiled. You're a lovely girl, you are.

Oh, I said, losing the argument.

Pylons whirred overhead. As we sat, our eyes got easy with the darkness and I saw a piece of greyish-white plastic whipping up and down on the hedge. The movement was making me panicky.

I felt quite nervous with him, because he wasn't looking at me, he was thinking all the time and I was used to all those unthinking men with their straight-forward hard-ons.

I'm sorry, he said.

You don't have to be, I told him.

I didn't want to make you feel bad.

I don't feel anything, I explained – and it was the honest truth – I can't feel where my body ends and the rest begins. I don't feel things any more. Not in that way, the way you're meaning.

He looked at me for the first time. Always? he said. Is that always the case? Or just because of what I said?

It's not because of what you said at all, I began to tell him – then I stopped speaking and wondered what the truth was. He'd unnerved me in some way.

I shivered and he turned the heater on. I like you Amy, he said, I didn't think I would, but I do.

I'm a slag, I said, mostly to put him off but also because it was the truth.

Don't say that, he said.

Would you like to lie on top of me? I asked him.

No – he looked pained – I'd crush you – look at the size of me.

I don't think you're fat, I said, And I can take it.

I put out my hand and touched his, which was still on the wheel. I didn't know why I was doing it, but it was so warm, so much warmer and more alive than mine. I wondered if the rest of him was warmer too.

OK, I went, What would you do if I was lying on you?

Oh God, he said, I'm trying to be honest with you. I think you at least deserve that.

83

I laughed, because it was a novel idea, the idea that I deserved something.

He started the car and we moved out of that electrified countryside. We did not speak again till he dropped me outside the flat, where he touched my hand again.

We won't tell him about this, he said – and I knew he meant Harris, not my husband.

I nodded, but I thought how out of hand everything was getting. First we had to tell Harris we'd been together when we hadn't, and then we had to say we hadn't when we had. And he said Harris was the one who told lies.

Five

It had seemed like chance that Gary and I should meet in the pub that night and had felt like choice when I fell for his big body and his gentle, unlikely ways.

But Harris had special skills. He had the skill of making you feel you were choosing, making you believe that anything could happen – that fate was just messing you around. They were good times, the ones that followed – though then I was too blinded by the newness to see it. Just when I thought I understood a fact, another, stranger one appeared. Like the dolls you get that you open and there's another inside – each one eating up the next, so as the whole thing can continue.

I knew what I seemed to have. I didn't know what was to come, but since when did anyone know the end of their story? But I always did have a craving for the next thing. My husband said it was one of my biggest weaknesses.

March was especially sunny, cheering you, conning you that spring had really arrived.

The air was moist. When the sun slid from between the clouds, it heated up your cheeks, wrists, shoulders for a few seconds. And everything in the Garden was in bud – a proper, noticeable cleanness in the air, light blue shadows on the leaves. You could smell sap and the squeak of life – plus the faintest whiff of bleach from the toilets.

The restaurant was busy, full of people who'd got their pay checks and been shopping and stowed their carrier bags under the tables. Cardigans were strewn on seats, older couples touching fingertips, gazing into each other's eyes. Hetty ran around with red cheeks, shouted at Jack who shouted back. Business was good. Sunshine made people want to have sex with each other, and that meant longish lunches and bigger tips, so we all did well out of it.

In all of March I think I only took two or three men round to Mara's, each one nervous and hard-faced and dying for a submissive mouth in which to stow their cocks. They were business types, salesmen maybe – blokes who spent their days in smoke-thick cars, with boxes and files of stuff and a spare jacket jiggling on a hook above the door.

They phoned head office on their mobiles and then went to the pub for a microwave lunch or stopped off at a garage for a Fanta or a chocolate bar. They had white stomachs that they didn't bother to suck in, blue stipple of stubble round their open mouths. They thought themselves so great, with their briefcases and their dirty bedroom talk. Maybe it was that I'd smartened up my appearance – a hair trim, a dab of blusher – but I seemed to be attracting posh types.

Their cocks exploded just like anyone else's. And then they tucked them back inside the shiny, man-made fabric of their pants.

Afterwards, I'd go down the building society, fill in the paying-in slip with the ballpoint on its silvery chain. The room was beige and soft and smelled of money and wide desks and clean, crumpled paper. I'd got close on three grand in my account, and it was earning interest for me all the while. No one had any idea what a big-time business woman I was getting to be.

*

Harris and I walked in Isabella Circus. The sky was mauve and crammed with cloud and a single poor bird was perched on a branch, telling us that any moment it might rain. I felt sorry watching its little chest shuddering with air and noise.

I've noticed a big improvement in Gary, he said. Since you and he – well, he's calmer for one thing.

My stomach went hot as I wondered how Harris knew. Gary swore he'd said nothing, kept up the pretence of not caring, and I'd barely spoken to him in front of Harris.

You're good for him, he said, almost proudly. I told you he needed a girlfriend.

I didn't look at him and I said nothing. What should I say to him about this?

Don't be angry, he went, I'm just glad to see him happy, that's all.

I said, You always try to make out Gary's someone to pity.

He made a shocked face. I never said that –

OK, that he needs help – support, whatever you like. Harris shrugged.

And he says roughly the same about you, I said.

Does he? he said quickly. Does he really? In what way?

Oh, I said, getting bolder, That I'm not to challenge the things you say, whether or not they're true –

He calls me a liar?

I jumped at the fierceness of his face, remembered Gary begging me not to have this conversation.

Not in so many words, I said.

He smiled, his face suddenly crabby and sly. You should know us by now, he said. You must make that judgement.

What judgement?

Which of us is telling the truth.

I tried to think about what he was saying, but my aggravation kept getting in the way. We turned the corner of Larch Street, past the Blue Jay Launderette and the Party Shop where there were balloons with clown faces on.

Look, said Harris, Gary has problems – has had problems. You can't blame me. You know I never tried to hide that from you.

There you go again.

This was old ground. When I'd challenged Harris, told him how Gary had denied everything, he'd looked hurt, but unsurprised. He said I had to believe him – that I did have a brother. And Gary's mother had gone off and left him.

Of course he won't own it, he said sadly. For a long time I didn't know how to handle that, it was all so new to me. He was very young – maybe it was his way of coping with what had happened. Rejection – especially by a parent – is never straightforward, it's a messy business. You can't fill the gaps and maybe you shouldn't try. I tried for a while and then I left it. I went with him. As he grew older I began to wonder whether I'd done him harm by allowing it.

Allowing what?

His, well, his peculiar vision of things – if he wanted something to be a certain way, he could almost make himself, and me, believe it was. You must admit that Gary's somehow different – he never says or does what you'd expect.

I didn't respond. Words and ideas were circling in my head, making me dizzy. Harris laid an arm across my shoulder, turned my face to his, so close I could smell the coffee on his breath.

I care for him, Amy, he said, I care for you both.

One day he whipped a piece of proof out of his wallet:

a snap of him feeding the toddler Gary – a faded baby with two teeth and a small fattish face.

I laughed because it was so obviously Gary – the troubled eyes, the little, flattened nose. You thought the older, bigger Gary was going to burst out at any moment, leaving the baby skin in a soft, pushed-off heap on the floor. He had on a stained bib and had turned the bowl of food upside down on his head. There was tomato in his hair and stuff on his face. Harris looked cool, delighted, tired, and full of himself. The shadow of a beard made him seem kind and unprepared. He held the spoon up like he knew he was having his picture taken.

Then I looked again.

It's just a baby, I said. It could be any baby.

He shook his head at me as if I was a sad case.

You carry that around?

He laughed shyly.

It doesn't prove anything, I told him. So you knew Gary as a baby – so what? He doesn't deny that you knew his parents.

Harris curled his lip.

He looked at the picture again like it might have something new to say to him, then he put it away.

You can believe what you like, he said. It makes no odds in the end. I say one thing, Gary says another. Poor Amy, what can you do? Look, you're free. You can walk away from both of us right now if you want.

Gary laughed when I told him.

He has a picture of a fat baby? Does it look like me?

A bit, I had to admit.

And does that make you trust me less?

I don't know, I said because I mostly told Gary the truth.

Does it change what you can feel is between us?

I shook my head.

If I tell you something, Gary said, Can you keep it absolutely to yourself?

OK, I said.

The other day, he said, I found something out.

I looked at him.

I found out that Harris hasn't lived here twenty years as he says. He moved here last year, from somewhere else.

I shivered, as if I was the one being found out.

How do you know?

Someone came into the bookshop, Gary said. We were chatting and it turned out they knew the people who lived in the house before. In fact, they still own it. Harris is renting off them.

You didn't know this? I asked him, even though I could tell the answer from his face.

Why do you think he came here, to this city? Gary asked me.

Bits of the truth were all around me, but I ignored them. I don't know, I said, like it was a Christmas quiz or something. Why did he?

I knew what Gary was going to say, but I wanted to turn away and not hear it.

I think he came here to look for you, he said. I think he came here because you were here.

And you? I said. Why did you come here?

Gary's face went quiet. That's another story, he said.

Are you going to ask him – about this?

Gary looked worried. No, he said. And you must promise me you won't either. He doesn't know we know and it's better that way. I don't mean you should worry about it – just carry on. Consider it a game. It'll just be interesting, to see what he does.

Interesting? I shivered again, at all this finding out. I'd not built my life on words, or books, or truth or lies. I wasn't clever like Gary, and I couldn't collect all the possibilities together in my head for long enough to work out what was what. All I had was my own feelings to go by and right now I felt stretched tight between these two strange men who had broken into my life, believing one and then the other, having a go at believing both. Sometimes I thought I'd burst with it.

He lied, I said. He came here specially.

I tell you something, Gary said, I'm glad he did.

And he twitched with laughter – he seemed to find the whole thing funnier than I did – and I felt his laugh somewhere up near my cervix because he was lying beneath me at that moment, his face against mine, his cock stuck in, tongue touching my lips, hands pinning me against him, holding me so he could go deeper if he liked. Which he did.

If I gasped, he smiled tenderly and withdrew a little; if I relaxed, he looked into my face and pushed.

Sex between me and the fat man had finally come about.

It had started back in February, a week or so after we met in the pub, with him opening a couple of beers in the bloody freezing office above the shop.

Cheers, he said, shoving papers on the desk aside to make space for the bottles. He wrinkled his nose and drank.

There wasn't much room, what with the calor gas heater and the big old desk and some of those wooden push-along steps and on the floor boxes and boxes of books – old ones with the covers coming off and more books piled up against the door and the walls. The smell was muck and dust and ash and ink. Week-old pizza crusts were growing mould on a paper plate on the grey metal filing cabinet.

I run a tidy ship, as you can see, he said.

What are they all? I said, meaning the books.

Waiting for me to go through them, he said. New acquisitions. Some will be dross, of course. Most, in fact.

I wiped the neck of the bottle with my sleeve. Why buy them, then?

I emptied a house. It's cheap enough. People die, no one wants to be bothered with sorting all the books. You don't know what you're going to get. Part of the fun is not knowing.

I must've made a face because he added, I like it, not knowing. Some people wouldn't. You probably wouldn't.

I don't like not knowing, I agreed.

You like to know what's going on, where you stand. You don't take chances. You haven't had enough to experience the luxury of taking chances.

Had enough of what? I asked him, thinking he was out of order telling me what I had and hadn't had.

Anything, he said, Enough of anything. He came over and stood very near me. I wanted him to touch me and I didn't, so I pretended not to notice.

I swigged my beer, then glanced at my watch. Ten past five and I had to be on at six. I'd come to him instead of going home between shifts.

Gary said, Do you mind if I ask you something?

Go ahead, I said.

I don't know how to put it.

Take your time, I said, holding the bottle neck tight so my hands wouldn't tremble.

Can I touch you?

Where?

Anywhere.

I laughed. I don't know, I said, realising that was a yes.

92

He must've been near because I could smell the good smell of his hair and the mannish-grease smell of his ears and nose and the beer-freshness of his saliva. He was breathing on me, close as a kiss, and where was I?

I shivered and put out a hand to feel his face, to feel the part of his round cheek just under the eye where the skin was interestingly bluish and nervy and nearly see-through.

Say something, he said and I was trying to think of what to say when he pulled me on his knee and rucked up my skirt and slid my knickers to the side and put his fingers inside me, gently pressing. The room went hot and I gasped.

How many is that? I asked him when I'd got my breath – because it felt a lot.

Only two, he said, his voice gone catchy and low. Want more?

I said nothing, so he put one more in and I felt myself stretching for him – and then another.

Better? he said.

I nodded, I could not speak, I was so wide, so taken up with the hardness of his fingers inside me. He waggled them gently and my skin swerved and went soft, like there was no divide between my clothed body and his. I was leaking into him, cotton, synthetics, hair and skin.

When he kissed me, I was already so keen I almost came. The kissing was so mouth to mouth, two sudden shapes pressing together that ought to have been across the room from each other.

He opened my legs a little more – the gentleness was killing me, so hard to bear – and he brought me up to the darkly tight place where you're on the edge, not wanting to go over or it will stop.

You're just how I thought you'd be, he breathed.

93

How? I gasped.

In there. He moved his fingers again and it made a wet noise and I sucked in book-smelling air.

He must have shifted a box or something because books were toppling – slap, slap – dust was shifting. I opened my eyes and saw the air full of fuzzy floating bits. He nudged my lips with his tongue and I resisted at first and then I opened them a bit.

And then I came.

Afterwards, he struck his fingers in my mouth to give me the salt-pee taste and, like a love film in reverse, he said sadly, We don't love each other, do we?

I laughed. I moved to his cock, wanting to give him some pleasure, but he gripped my hand to stop me.

Another time.

He was picking up the books which had fallen. He showed me one, held it out. It was hard and dark brown with a polythene cover.

I thought it was a first edition, he said, But it has a fucking library plate in it, look.

I stared lazily, still warm and loose from the come. So?

So it's worthless. He flung it down behind the desk.

But you could still read it?

He laughed. I don't read all these books. Anyway, I wouldn't want to – it's been in some pissy library, in and out of people's houses –

Sticky fingers, I said.

He laughed loudly.

Shall we do it again? I asked him, getting on him like a pony and lacing my fingers round his big, fat neck.

What, now?

Not now, I have to go to work.

You're lovely, you are, he said, placing the palms of his hands on my ribs like a guitar getting ready to play. I've never done this.

94

Never done what? I said – but he just kissed my fingers – We'll do it tomorrow? I suggested.

Okay, he whispered, But don't tell Harris.

When I got home that night, my husband was sitting up in bed waiting for me, hands bunched together around a glass of Madeira. He loved those sticky adult drinks – the ones you have a tiny measure of and the rest gets dusty on a shelf.

Someone from work saw you in the Garden for the Blind, he said in a fake-jolly voice, Talking to a man!

I sat down heavily on the rumpled edge of the bed. I was tired – tired from fucking and from thinking and from serving food. It was late. Spice and fat smells were in my hair. My eyes pricked with tiredness, my legs ached, all I wanted was sleep.

A man? I said, surprised it should come up now, just when I'd been less busy in that department.

A red-haired bloke, he said, Thickset apparently. It was some while ago – he didn't know whether he should tell me. Then he decided it was only fair I know what's what.

I listened to him and said nothing. He didn't scare me with his careful little, pricked-out sentences.

It's possible, I said slowly. I do sometimes go and sit there if I've some time between shifts. I don't remember any man, though.

Strange, said my husband, Considering you left together.

I laughed, got up then, walked to the chest and took my earrings off, plink, plink in the saucer.

Then they saw someone else, I said. Why would I leave with a man?

He zapped on the TV, sipped his drink, with all the mean, small thinness of a man seen straight after the beauty and bigness of Gary.

95

That's not the question, he said. No, the question is, if you were going to fuck someone else, why would you choose some ugly fucker with a beer belly?

It does seem surprising, I said and pulled off my clothes.

It does, yes, he said, agreeing with himself.

He fucked me then. You could say I was asking for it, showing myself to him with no clothes on like that. As his hands touched and parted my thighs, I thought of what Gary's fingers had done and got slippery on the idea, and then felt ashamed to be dividing myself in this way.

After the other one had come, he lay there on top of me for a moment till I couldn't breathe any more and then he saved me by rolling off and suddenly said, in a voice edged with kindness, Are you all right, Amy?

I'm fine thanks, I said.

How can you like me? I ask him, After all the things you know?

You are an innocent, Gary says. There are things about me he could tell you too. I mean it. Maybe he will.

We are on a bench in Henrietta Park, side by side like two old folk and now he pulls me round so my head's heavy in his lap, my laced-up feet touching the far end of the bench. I feel the action of blood in my body, smell the air, wispy with bonfire.

Do you like fucking? he asks me in his oddly definite voice. Do you really like it? You can tell me the truth now.

The truth? I hold up my wool hands, spread the fingers and glimpse neat, light slices of sky through them. Not really, I say, I prefer to know what's going on and you can't ever properly know with sex.

What's to know?

96

I mean to be prepared, to know what's coming.

You don't like surprises?

That's right, I agree. Surprises are bad. I mean it.

I know you do. You're scared someone will hurt you?

My heart dips and contracts. That's right, I say again.

He thinks about this. And does this apply to me? he asks. To what we do?

I close my eyes, can't feel if I'm smiling or not. I like your fingers, I say.

But that's not fucking, is it, what I do with my fingers? He is pulling off my gloves and feeling my hands so stiff and chapped from peeling veg and from the suds we wash the glasses in at work.

What's fucking? I ask him then. One thing going in another – in and out for fun? What does fucking matter? I like it when you do things.

Things?

You know –

Say it, he whispers, Say what I do. He's still playing with my fingers, moving them, one at a time.

I can't, I say, laughing.

Don't be embarrassed.

I can't.

Those men, he says then. Did you take them to hotels?

Not hotels, I say, shocked at his not knowing. How would I afford hotels?

How much did they pay you?

The conversation has turned. I sit up and put my gloves back on. How do you know it's over? I might still be doing it, I say.

He looks at my face, pushes his fingers through my hair.

You might still be, is all he says.

I fall against his body and it turns all emotional, with kisses that we haven't had before – kisses which ask for something back in return. I shiver even though I'm jacketed in wool like a fucking sheep.

Threads are unravelling in my gut, blood pumping. I lick the fat bareness of his fingers. They taste of his shop and that calms me down, reminds me of our sex.

April. I thought I really had more or less given up my thing of fucking for money, but the ginger-haired man caught up with me on Bennett Street one day towards the end of the month and offered me twice as much as before.

You can come with me to a machine, get some cash, he said.

I don't know.

I was nervous that someone would spot us. I wasn't even sure if Mara's was free. I hadn't been there since the businessmen and she always had plenty of girls who wanted the space.

Go on, he said. He didn't try to touch me, he kept his distance. I like you, Vicky, you're my type. It's a bit of a temptation, coming across you on the street like this.

I'm not Vicky, I said.

Whatever. Come on, come and get the fucking money with me.

What do you want? I asked him, looking at the blue-whiteness of his face, the bulging vein that throbbed in his forehead. He looked dirty. Maybe he was a builder. There was plaster dust on his sagging jeans and a newspaper sticking out of his back pocket.

The same, he said, Exactly the frigging same as before. Twice the money. I'm not kidding.

I looked at him a moment and figured that if he wanted it that much he'd be so desperate he'd come almost immediately. That meant I'd be getting roughly four times as much, minute for minute. Okay, I said and we turned and walked back over the bridge.

You live around here, Vicky? he asked me.

Mind your own business, I said.

Only asking.

He smiled, dazed, like I'd woken him out of sleep. There were several people waiting at the machine. It would be just my luck to meet some colleague of my husband's. Or else Gwen, out shopping, pink-faced and glassy-eyed. But he put in his card quickly and the money came out and we probably looked like any other couple, him tucking it in his wallet, me trotting along by his side.

Mara had a red, wet cold and not much under her robe which could frankly have done with a wash. She had the TV going – you could see its blue jumpy light through the crack in her door.

Long time no see, she said without so much as looking at him and she put me in the dark little back room, to make a point, I suppose. The fluorescent tube light had been knocked off the ceiling, so you only had what greenish light came in from the side window. There were long black hairs on the carpet, a tube of hand cream on the bedside table, with squeezes in it. I took the money off him first and folded it into my bag.

I took a condom from the drawer, but he didn't even let me get down on my knees or unzip him. Instead he pushed me straight back on the little single bed, sitting his whole weight on my chest and forcing my mouth open with his fingers. I hadn't heard him unzip, but he must've because straightaway the naked cock was in – half soft, half hard – pushing, bending into the side of my cheek, its silky skin grazing my teeth, then the hot, rounded bulk of it jamming down my throat.

I struggled, choking, plucking at his clothes, but he seemed to like that – seemed to want to do it more. I felt his arse jiggling on my rib cage, thighs nudging at my breasts. Then one of his hands held both my wrists, the other clawed at my bra, got out a nipple and pinched it.

My breath moving up, hot and broken in my chest as he came, the bitterness of his sex pooling in the edges of my cheeks as I twisted my face so as not to choke.

Then a moment of nothing. His eyes closed, the lids lilac, smooth as a child's. He gets off me roughly, using my shoulder to lever himself off the bed.

He says nothing, but his eyes are suddenly on me as he grabs his newspaper and jacket and goes. He could have taken back his money, but he doesn't.

I spit and spit on to Mara's grubby bedspread, the flavour holding on hard to my tongue. After a moment's lying there shaking, I sit up, vomit, cry – and leave before Mara can call me in for a chat.

Life is hard, my foster father Brian used to say. It's not supposed to be easy. What's so special about you, Amy, that you should expect to breeze through it?

Brian measured everyone's lot against his own – he was the sort to follow a meal with his eyes as it was brought to the table, furtively compare another person's slice of apple pie with his. He was full of meanness – he said life wasn't fair. He went on and on about all the exams he'd worked for in his life, all the qualifications, like he held you personally responsible or something.

His eyes were moist with self-love. He had been a choirboy and had life-saving medals, but he never looked much like an angel, nor saved anyone's life. He read from the Bible and cried in churches. He knew the names of poets and people who did oil paintings and he wore bicycle clips and, now and then, a bowler hat. He respected people with letters after their name. He said money was not important, but he grovelled whenever he met or spoke about anyone who had some. He aspired to social standing, he wanted to be Lord of the Manor and dripping in inherited gold, but deep down he was mean. You are the child of adoptive parents, he told me, You've landed on your feet, but don't expect to profit financially. He seemed to find it disgusting and exciting that my mother had been a teenager when she had me.

Sundays, he'd take us bowling, Sally and me and sometimes Freddy. The stadium smelled of feet and all you heard was the thud, thud, thud as the skittles went down. You had to hire soft, two-tone shoes that never fitted and I always made a big fuss about wearing them and ended up in just my socks. I wouldn't show my naked feet to anyone – it just felt dirty, too much like sex. And I didn't want other people's sweat on me and I didn't like sticking my fingers in the ball holes either.

It seemed stupid, that a man like Brian went bowling. He wasn't any good at it. He just liked putting on those stinking shoes. That and the pleasure of knocking something down.

I go straight home – the house is empty except for Megan. My husband is thankfully out on a call.

After gargling with some antiseptic, I run a hot bath, not bothering with any stuff in it. I pull my body down under the water, rolling and churning, taking in the bubble sounds in the orangey-pretend darkness.

I can go heavy, hold my head down, but I can't find the nerve to breathe in water. It's nature – you have to come up, join in the fight for air, however much you hate yourself. You think you'll resist that next breath but the body has other ideas.

If I could leave this world now without going through the business of forcing out life, I'd do it. No pain, no fuss, no second chance. There ought to be a switch. So many would pull it.

Tea, said Harris as we walked on Lansdowne Crescent – a half-circle of houses so high and all the same against the wide, flat sky they made you dizzy – I'm going to buy you tea at the Majesty. My treat. I insist.

The Majesty had plushy plum carpets and a lift with a cage door which clanked across when you got in, and you paid through the nose for bits of cress and thin, frail biscuits smelling of butter and fresh air.

Old rich people stayed at the Majesty. They walked around and whispered to each other in the powdery silence or they downed their sherry and fell asleep in an upright position and some of them had coats made of fur.

I'm not hungry, I said.

You're going to eat. Sandwiches or whatever there is.

In the hotel drawing-room, all you heard was ticking, all you saw was old brown wood and paintings. Even the mirrors had a grey skin of oldness on them, your face was dusted over with it if you peered in. A boy waiter brought egg mayo sandwiches with the crusts cut off and scalding Darjeeling in a heavy silver pot with extra water on the side. He had on his black and whites but you could see DMs peeping out from under the trousers.

There were several quiet old people in the room, but Harris wasn't fussed. He rolled a cigarette, balancing his stuff on a *Country Life* spread on his knees. There was a pile of newspapers, mostly the flesh-coloured money one. The pink velvet of my armchair was rubbed away to show a fat grainy texture much like skin and I couldn't help stroking it. That brought on the feeling I was going to vomit. Ever since the naked prick in my mouth I'd been feeling queasy.

Do me a roll-up, I said to Harris as I went off to the Ladies.

I won't pour till you're back, he promised.

I thought how married we sounded.

Downstairs, the carpets were dark and rosy, and little pump things of hand cream stood by the lit-up mirrors. A blank-faced girl moved up and down the row of basins spraying and wiping.

It was so quiet down there you could hear her breathing. I didn't like to go with someone listening, so I put paper down the loo to dull the sound. I emptied from both ends, wiped my mouth on toilet paper, flushed and then squirted my purse atomiser into the air to take away the smell.

There were fresh flowers in white vases, dropping their bright orange pollen on the marble top. As you washed, the girl hung around behind you and wiped the little specks of water from round the basin when you'd finished.

I put ten pence in the saucer and hoped she wouldn't know which was mine as there were some twenties and a fifty in there. Ta, she said, leaning against the basins watching me.

Is it hot in here or is it me? I asked her.

It's you, she said and blew the dead-looking wisps of hair off her face.

Upstairs, he was walking up and down, making a show of looking at the pictures on the walls.

He passed me my cigarette and I lit it off his, but I took one drag and realised I couldn't smoke it. It felt like there was ash piling up inside me already and I was going to gag. Sorry, I said, stubbing it on a poncey little decorated saucer.

What is it?

Nothing. Thought I wanted one but I don't.

You need to eat, he said.

I don't think I can.

Force yourself, Amy – I'm going to see that you eat something.

I mean it, I can't.

Are you ill?

I don't think so.

What are you, then?

I don't know, I said.

He looked at the sandwiches and carried on blowing out smoke and looking at me, and after a moment or two he began to laugh again.

You think your secrets are your own concern, but even old Mensa-brain Paula had been taking notes.

Hmm, she goes, What is it, Amy? Something's different about you.

Different?

Your face, I don't know – softer – around your mouth. And you're wearing liner. Do you know what I think it is?

Amaze me.

I'm just folding napkins, running my fingers slowly over the stiff linen, folding, plumping the pile and starting another. Seeing the perfect piles lined up gives me little shocks of pleasure.

I think you're having an affair.

She puts a little fanfare on the words, as if saying them makes them possible, even true.

I laugh.

So? she goes.

I can't really say.

Can't say because I'm right?

No, I tell her, You're wrong.

Gwen yells, Has someone taken the Budweiser to the window table? Paula takes it. When she comes back she says, You're a funny girl, Amy. So bloody secretive, keeping it all in. Don't you ever tell anybody what you're up to? I had an affair once, you know. It wasn't such a big deal.

Who says I'm having an affair?

It's nothing to be ashamed of, Amy.

Who was your affair with? I ask her, suddenly interested.

Oh, no one, just a man I met. I told Ron in the end.

You told him?

He didn't mind. He knows me. He knew it meant nothing.

Then why do it? What's the point of being married?

I'm just telling you what's what, she says, I can't give you a reason. I don't know what I'm doing half the time, let alone why – what about you?

I smile – think of what I've done recently – for reasons I've barely gone into. I don't know, I say.

Then Gwen says that number thirty-four is ready and away and if Paula's having a mid-life crisis, she'd better do it out of Hetty's earshot because there are looks coming our way.

I finish the napkins and go in the toilet – wash my hands with the pink soap, dry them with a paper towel, give myself a long looking over. I push my hair back behind my ears, lick my lips. Does it show, then? Has the fat man somehow printed himself on my face? I remember his little, soft kisses, think of how his fingers poking in and out make me float – high, high, higher.

When there's nothing more to think, I sit down on

the closed toilet seat, light a fag and look for split ends in my hair. Find hardly any.

Next day, Gary and I meet up after the lunch shift, go into the toy department of Lilley's where he buys me a small pink plastic heart on a strong thin white cord of the type you use to pull curtains shut. 89 pence, in the pocket money section. We also get two bubble pots with wands at 99 pence each.

Cheapo, he says, fixing the heart round my neck.

I kiss it. The plastic's hard and warm and shiny against my lips. He kisses me – hot and swimmy – and I hope my hair doesn't stink of frying.

We blow the bubbles off Chantney Bridge. The sun goes in and out, doing these amazing effects with the soap. The bubbles carry flashes of pink, purple, green and yellow in them. They quiver and bulge. One rests on the brown water for a moment before bursting. Some stick together in the air for a second or two, then burst as if they've never existed.

I hold on to his big fat hand and think that what we're doing feels so easy and good it must be dangerous.

You don't trust anyone, do you? he says, as if he can climb inside my head and sort the different parts and read them aloud to a gathered audience.

On the parapet of the bridge, two hunched-up birds sit watching us with fed-up faces.

Life with my husband had shrunk to something small and pinched and sad.

My perfect evening was to get in a deep hot bath and shave my legs and go to bed alone with a magazine, a can of Lilt and a bag of crisps. If I was working, I sometimes made him something and left it in the fridge, or else I just got a chop or a piece of fish and left him to it.

Often I needn't have bothered because he went out anyway. I could tell by how clean the kitchen was when I got home. Sometimes he just had Pot Noodles or took Megan and went out to the Kebab shop. Sometimes he said that's where he'd been but he was gone a hell of a long time for just around the block.

He was the kind of person who'd sit in the pub alone, doing the crossword, and get talking to someone else who was doing the exact same thing.

One night he got talking to someone who lived up Melly Hill way.

Met a bloke who reckons he knows that old boyfriend of your mum's, he said as he clipped on Megan's lead for her late-night walk.

Oh? My face let me down by going red. My husband didn't know how much I was seeing Harris, or Gary. He knew nothing and for the moment I wanted to keep it that way. But my husband didn't look at my face.

Well, not knows, he said, Knows of.

Oh yeah?

Yeah. He said he hasn't lived here very long at all, your man. Said he arrived from abroad with a couple of suitcases and that's it. Matter of months he'd been there, this bloke said.

Oh, I know, I said quickly, I know that.

You told me he'd been here for years, my husband said. I thought that was what was supposed to be so weird about it all?

I know. I got it wrong.

Wrong?

I don't know what you're getting at, I said.

And you said he was your mum's boyfriend, but according to this chap he's, well, he's not exactly straight –

I laughed, I was really amused. I don't think he's gay, I said.

Lives with another bloke, doesn't he?

Gary? His lodger – they're just friends.

That's what they told you, was it? said my husband, and he clicked his teeth at Megan and let himself out the back door.

Next day he was so full of himself. He'd given up on married life. He microwaved food and zapped channels. He was studying for some exams which would amount to a promotion if he passed.

Don't touch anything, he said, if I approached the living-room table, Don't move a fucking thing.

His papers and files were in thick, overlapping layers all over everything. He got furious if I tried to tidy up.

Why would I want to touch your bloody papers?

Megan came and pushed her wet, fishy nose into my hands. I shoved her away.

He ignored me. He was writing in a ring-binder file and at the same time watching a TV programme about real-life murders police have solved. A student was killed by a canal on a hot night. They showed a photo of her at a pub with her friends – blonde crimped hair and red dots in her eyes and a big, ecstatic smile on her face. Murder victims always look like they were enjoying life. There are no snaps anywhere of me looking that happy.

Come here, he said and tried to touch my legs and bum.

He wanted us to try for a family, but I imagined a kid that was a human cocktail of all our grief. Or else I pictured it born a spastic or something and us two yoked together for life by the tragedy and ongoing terribleness of it.

So I always coaxed a condom on to his eager, pur-plish, stretched-out dick. He complained he didn't feel like a husband, and he fucked me without tenderness or comment and afterwards he eased the thing off and carried all his rejected seed into the bathroom at arm's length.

Mostly I sat with them in the sunny, dusty room at Melly Hill – the place I always ended up when I escaped from the deadness of our flat on Sundays.

Where did he think I went? I didn't care, I didn't want to consider. As I stepped out the door, he melted to nothing – and I moved in my secret world, unaccountable and scary and free.

The dog was not on my side. She made a point of being restless at Melly Hill – despite the longish walk and dog chocs and general fuss made of her. She wouldn't settle – skirted the edges of the room, dusting the tops of books with her tail and finally flopped down by the fire, evil eyes fixed on my hands. Then a curl of her black lip, a dirty, pointed sigh. As if she knew what a tart I was.

I wanted Gary to think I liked Megan – that here was a girl who was kind to animals – but privately, I was mean. I whispered in her ear that she was a dumb bitch, that she had fish breath. I pinched her ears and told her I was glad she couldn't run off and shop me to her beloved, bloody master.

April in England is so awfully fucking nice. Just when you're losing hope, there it is, the whole world curling up and grinning its head off at you.

In the neglected garden at Melly Hill, everything's enlarged, grown so big you can't dismiss it now. Clean, baby shoots everywhere, pussy willow pressing against the watery sky, acidic grass blades growing, dumb, determined little flowers budding in the wet, black beds.

Gary and I are standing on the bright lawn. In the

sun, his size looks more like generosity – exotic, dark and definite. I watch with pleasure as he frowns and eats a banana.

Look, watch out for Harris, he says, Now more than ever.

Why? – I say it in a flat voice.

Truly, Amy, if I could tell you I would. I don't want to be enigmatic and all that crap. I've never loved anyone more than you. I don't want you to go away.

Why should I go away?

You're not going anywhere. I couldn't have you leave me now.

I'm not going anywhere, I whisper to him, my voice quieter than the chatter of the birds.

I know, he says, and squeezes the end of the banana into his big mouth and holds the skin, dangling.

I've never loved anyone, I begin to tell him – and I find I want to say more but I have a bad habit of blocking the words just as I'm getting started.

He looks at my face and puts his arms around me, still holding the banana skin. Hugging him, I smell its sweet, babyish smell.

Harris is inside, rolling a fat joint, watching us probably.

We go in and I sit there in the big chair with my sneakered feet on the table saying anything that comes into my head. Sometimes I tell stories – flashes of memory from the island. Harris corrects me or joins in. Sometimes I tell jokes and Gary always laughs when I get the endings wrong. Sometimes I say nothing, enjoy the luxury of the different sorts of silence.

Tell us all about your week, Harris will go, and I'll entertain him with the fuckwit customers we've had or the evenings when we've been run off our feet or how Mervyn went and slipped in some fish grease and fractured his wrist and had to have gas for the pain.

They know all about Paula's head rash and how Karen is thinking of going back to the States though her husband isn't keen and how *Gourmet* magazine came to photograph the tapas table after I did it, and who knows, I might even get a credit when it comes out?

As we get more stoned, we move closer together and the muscles in my arms and legs go smooth, the boundaries between our bodies dive and blur. If Harris leaves the room for a moment, Gary's body leaks into mine. A single glance from him makes the space between my thighs go fizzy.

Gary acted like I was his girlfriend, married or not. He hadn't gone on about love – maybe he knew that wasn't the way to make me his – but he'd made it clear he was counting on certain things, waiting, if you like.

Harris won't like it, he told me.

Won't like what?

You and me – the way we are now. He won't like it.

But, I said, He wanted it, it was his idea, remember? In the beginning.

In the beginning, yes, of course it was. When he had complete control. But now –

Now what? I asked him, remembering me and Harris in the Garden for the Blind and flushing.

You wait, Gary said. Just don't be surprised. Remember what I said.

Maybe he was right. Maybe Harris was fed up with him. I watched him preparing to bait Gary, circling him, eyeing him whilst pretending not to, shooting up close without warning. Such games gave me the creeps.

Which of us do you love the most? he asked me, stopping behind us as we sat on the sofa, placing his hand like a cap on the top of my head.

I love both of you.

Both equally?

Both equally, I lied, playing the game.

But if you had to choose?

I'd refuse. I couldn't choose.

But if you had to?

Then I'd choose no one. I'd run away.

This pleased Harris. He broke into amazed laughter. Aha! But we'd find you. We'd come and get you.

I'd leave her alone, said Gary quietly, She's been chased enough.

I saw Harris look sharply at him.

He loves me best, I tell Harris, to annoy him.

You're a naive man, Gary, an idiot, said Harris. Love is blind, selfishly optimistic, bursting with energy. Love doesn't give up. Love has its own good, its own satisfaction, in mind. Love fights. It doesn't always win but it never just sits back and says 'oh well' and does nothing.

Excuse me, I said, But what's all this about love? Who said I wanted it?

Women always want it, said Harris. What are you saying? That you know about women?

Shut up, Harris, said Gary with unexpected force.

Harris tried to speak but Gary ignored him and turned to me.

What do you want? he asked me.

I don't know, I said. Maybe a quiet life.

There was a pause. Harris blinked.

Six

Harris looked to spend time with me without Gary. He often called on me at work and waited upstairs till the end of the shift and sometimes we walked or went and sat in a pub together.

Sometimes we sat in easy, dumb silence, like family. I'd got used to the look of him, the obvious, bristled edges of his face, the sound of his breath as he did his thinking, made up his ideas. I was waiting – for what? For him to act? I don't know. Maybe. Perhaps.

It was almost summer when we passed the Garden for the Blind and that's why it was suddenly all in bloom, all that waxy colour in the light lateness of the afternoon. The twitter of birds, the hum of bees. The change was a shock to me.

Come – Harris linked his arm through mine – Let's pay homage.

He guided me in through the black wrought iron gate and sat us on a bench. It wasn't my bench. It was one of the ones right at the other end. So I felt he couldn't know and I was glad.

All these flowers, I commented at last.

He smiled. How long since you were here?

I flushed. Oh, ages, I said.

The trees had still been hard, brittle shapes, the air gluey with darkness, on the days I'd gone with all those men. It seemed another age. You couldn't be with a man like that on a sweet-smelling May evening, you couldn't bear to look at his cock in the clear light of summer.

I thought how I seemed to have a new self emerging and how it was clean and warm and unaffected by what I'd done in the long-ago winter. Second chances and all that.

I know when you were here, he said.

I didn't reply, I don't think he expected me to. He waited a moment, then he took my chin and tilted it, turned it towards him. His hands were hot for an old man, but then he was full of surprises.

Amy – he began and then broke off and looked at me.

You're not angry with me? I said.

How can you say that?

I thought –

Jesus Christ, he said, I'd love to know what you actually think.

But he wasn't asking. His hands were still on my chin and I suddenly knew I wanted him to keep them there. If he took them off, the world would turn cold, ideas that made temporary sense would slide away. I felt the shape of my own face, the complicated heaviness of my head. But he went and let go, dropped his fingers to his lap.

How did you let them know? he asked me, in a cool, quiet voice.

What?

That you'd do it.

I don't know, I said.

Don't be shy, he said, his eyes on the bed of flowers. You can tell me.

Tell you what?

There must have been some sign, something you did –

Maybe – I began.

114

His eyes flicked up to watch my face.

Maybe I – looked at them.

Looked at them?

I shrugged. You know – in a certain way.

And they'd come to you?

I saw how eager he was to know. I hesitated and bit my lip and pretended to inspect my fingers and then I said, Well, not always. Sometimes. Some were shy or scared at first –

Scared?

I don't know, it was a big deal, I suppose. Maybe it was their first time.

How did you know they weren't going to hurt you?

I didn't. I mean, some did.

He breathed out some air and looked away at the round circles of flowers which cut into the middle of the grass. Above us a plane was climbing with its dragging noise.

I pushed up my sleeves. It was hot in the garden. I looked at him and thought he had tears and was blinking them away and then I looked at him a second time and thought he actually didn't and maybe it was just what I'd hoped to see.

Jesus, fuck – he said.

I put my hand on his sleeve. Maybe they were tears.

I hate myself Amy, he said.

I know, I whispered – so quiet, he didn't have to hear me if he didn't want to.

No, you don't know, he said, You've no idea. I haven't always been honest with you –

Gary said – I began.

Forget Gary, he said bitterly, I don't want to know what Gary says.

He looked ready for me to be angry at him saying that about Gary, and that's when I knew I was going to kiss him. Sometimes a good long kiss is like taking a bite out of something: you don't need the whole thing – maybe you don't even want it – but you absolutely have to have a taste.

Or maybe it was that place – the Garden for the Blind – trees all in leaf and the air pink as sugar and Harris with unexpected freckles on his nose, and the men probably coming and going from the toilet and the traffic a permanent sing-song in the distance. Hyacinths in neat, bright circles in all the beds. Black soil, blue blooms, white pith – the most perfectly upright flower in the world: my cue to get on my feet.

So I stood in front of him as he sat on that bench in the place where I'd so easily given up so many parts of me and I took his shoulders in my hands and bent and put my mouth on his. It was like lighting a candle, slow, quivery, unlikely at first, then hot and amazing as it took effect.

My legs slid between his so as to get him closer.

At first his lips were simply there, and then, after I'd licked them, they were moving, wetting, taking shape and doing it back to me. It was so easy, kissing him. It wasn't like the beginnings of sex, but a whole thing in itself, complete and sorted and done. I was enjoying the rough pattern of his tongue, the glassiness of his teeth, the surprising flavour of his saliva, when he broke off suddenly, turned his head.

You're your mother's girl! Well, aren't you? Aren't you?

What?

I looked at him. He spoke sharply, spitting, his face dark with what I'd understood to be passion.

I don't want that rubbish from you, he said. What would Gary say if he knew you were offering me that?

I felt tears coming, but I held them in. I realised as I saw this change, saw him hating me, that I hadn't wanted him either. I'd done what I thought he wanted, what I thought I had to do.

That was disgusting, Amy, he said.

I'm sorry –

Bad girl. It would destroy Gary, if I told him what you just did.

Don't tell him, I said, Don't tell him.

We've just got Gary sorted, just got him on the straight and narrow and his girlfriend tries to –

Stop it, I said, I want to go.

Fine, he said, We'll go. And we both got up and walked out of the Garden. I considered running from him, but was afraid he'd go straight to Gary. So we walked, close together, like any couple. A breeze had started up and the blossom floated down around our heads like a pretend wedding.

Megan had got her tail bitten into somehow, silly mut. She hated the sharp, bleachy smell of the vet's, the scratchy lino which made her crouch down and whimper and wobble and sink to her knees as she walked.

Come on, Megs, I said, and I pulled hard on her lead but she wouldn't budge. So I tried to shove her fat hairy behind but she sat down and her back legs slid up from under her. Spit was hanging from the corner of her mouth where her lips were jagged and piebald pink. In the end I had to pick her up in my arms, her four legs sticking up in the air like furniture.

The vet trimmed away some dried blood and hair and then I held her while he swabbed it down with disinfectant and gave her a shot of antibiotic. She trembled.

When it was done, he washed his hands and gave me a foil pack of pills – a four-day course – and showed me how to get them down her. I wrote out a cheque for thirty quid. He waved away my card – I know you, he said, Take care. Bring her back if you have any worries.

My husband was waiting outside on a yellow line and straightaway Megan was all over him. He laughed and smoothed her hairy face with both hands, kissed her forehead.

Pills? he said.

Thirty quid, she cost us, your dog.

I handed him the pack and he sighed but you could tell he thought she was worth it. What do you do with her, where do you take her? he asked me.

She didn't get bitten when she was out with me, I said.

I don't know where you take her, he said again.

Megan put her ears flat and gave me a sour look.

Oh for fuck's sake, I said, She probably bites it herself.

He didn't laugh. I turned and stuck my tongue out at the dog. She looked away.

The city is drowning in sunshine, trees bending and lifting in the breeze, but in the evenings at Melly Hill, Harris – who doesn't seem to notice the seasons or weather – still makes a fire.

It's like he's forgotten the incident in the Garden – he's as friendly as he ever was. Some days he looks at me coolly and I worry that he's thinking things, but other days he's warm and kind as ever, and I feel stupid for having put him through what I did, ashamed of my whorish nature, afraid for Gary and me and what I'll do to trash the precious and surprising thing we have.

Gary doesn't seem to know anything, but I see him watching Harris, waiting.

I go with Gary to the supermarket because they need things.

118

Outside, at the trolley park, people are holding carrier bags and queueing for cabs, smoking cigarettes. I hold Gary's hand. I am pleased to think we look like any other couple. The supermarket at Melly Hill is bigger than the one I go to with my husband – safe because it's faraway, on the other side of the city. It has toilets and a dry cleaner's and a coffee shop.

I've never been shopping with Gary. You'd think he'd never been at all. He skips around, commenting on all the choice, the design, the pictures, the promises, as if it's all new to him. He puts in oranges and vodka and a bottle of champagne, a bulb of fennel – and then seems stuck.

Who does the shopping normally in your house? I ask him.

Guess, he says.

How old are you, Gary?

He chuckles, pulls out notes like they're foreign or toy ones, hands one too many to the cashier.

One day his car just stopped working and he left it in a lay-by. From then on we walked everywhere. I got a stitch and had to sit down on a bench by the bridge where pigeons were picking over a split bag of Quavers. He put his arm around me and told me that walking was good for the heart.

I told him that fucking was also good for the heart. He told me I was full of good sense and that's why he liked me.

My husband was still in the dark. Or maybe he wasn't, because one day he came out of the toilet after a longish read of the paper and smacked me in the face.

It sent me back, making me hit the chest of drawers on the landing, knocking off some towels and a half-full Coke can that splashed its brown drips on the carpet. I felt sweat prick under my arms and I waited while he went downstairs and into the kitchen. I followed and pulled a chair out and sat down. I tried not to tremble as it made my teeth click together in a dumb way. I clenched my mouth and recognised the sourness of no breakfast. It was the weekend and the radio was banging on about love. I leaned over and switched it off. What's going on? I said.

He just laughed – loudly, not his normal laugh.

The phone rang but the machine was on. I started to get up. Leave it, he snapped.

We listened as his voice came on all casual and smiley, saying to leave a message. It was someone from his mother's nursing home. Ring us, they said, it's urgent. A beep.

You'd better ring, I said, but he just stayed there, staring. Because I felt sorry for him, I passed him the phone, but it just sat there, next to the white lump of his fed-up hands.

You look at photos of your loved ones or the dead and you can't help it, you trawl for clues. In all the pictures, my mother-in-law is a fresh but bumpy young woman with hopeful, curving cheeks and lit-up eyes.

She's laughing – how could she be laughing, with all that mental illness and peas rolling under her wheelchair to look forward to in her future? You take in her checked cotton skirt, her patent shoes, her wet-look handbag, and you can't make things fit. You think it was a different person that got out of bed in the morning and put them on, doing up the buttons and straps, snapping the bag shut, the sun shining barmily in on her plans for the day.

My husband says he knew she hadn't long, but the death of your mum always comes as a shock.

Again and again after Harris gave it to me, I searched

that little photo of my mother for the facts of her life and her drowning, but there was never a single clue. No sign that she would leave me – walk into that glittery ocean without a backward glance.

I looked and looked, hoping to suck out a small taste of the truth, and all I saw was her perfectly relaxed face and the long, straight lie of her blonde hair.

I looked at Gary and saw he was staring out the window and there were tears rolling all down his face.

I turned to Harris. What's going on? I said, What's he crying for?

I felt rough and I quite liked it. I was sick of feeling sympathy for people.

He's crying for you, said Harris. He's upset that your husband laid into you like that. He doesn't want you to be hit.

I watched the fat man and didn't know whether I felt love or just annoyed that he made no effort to wipe the tears off his face. Soon they would run down and tickle the lobes of his ears, his neck, land on his shirt. I'd never seen a man cry, though I knew it happened. I wondered why I couldn't bring myself to say a nice thing.

You shouldn't feel sorry for me, I told them both, My husband's mother just died and he's a bit shook up right now. He hasn't hit me before and I don't expect him to do it again. And maybe he's got a point. Maybe I've been out of the house too much recently –

You don't believe that, Gary interrupted his crying to say quickly.

You don't know what I believe, I told the two of them. You think you know me pretty well, but you don't. I only met you a few months ago. We hardly know each other.

I think I said that – it's what I wanted to say, anyway.

Harris smiled and Gary – well I didn't bother looking to see what he did.

Instead, I went into their bare, boys' kitchen and put on the kettle. There were dirty things everywhere, food spilling out of packets, milk going off, dust and dead insects on the windowsill.

The sun was out, shining hotly, blotting up the dust which fell and sparkled. I laughed to myself as if the weather was ridiculous, but it wasn't the weather I was laughing at and I wasn't really laughing.

And then one day I run into Mara, on the edge of the shopping precinct in front of the Abbey, where a pack of Brownies are doing song and dance numbers from *Salad Days*.

On her arm are one or two old carrier bags and she's wearing sunglasses, the morning brightness showing up the bad skin and the lines from so much doing it for money. She's been on the game for years and you can tell by the roughness of her, the sad heaviness, the way she doesn't care how her body hangs out of her clothes.

I expect her to be angry with me for not coming in, but she just says hi and that she's been wondering how I was getting on.

I tell her I'm sorry I haven't been in touch and then I start to explain about my mother-in-law's passing away and that, except she's not really listening.

Did you know we were busted? she tells me. Some sneaky old bugger had been watching the house, knew all our comings and goings –

I don't have to pretend – I'm really shocked. Mara's was so discreet. But she says not to worry, puts down her shopping and delves in her bag for a card – pale pink with an address printed on it.

My new place, wait till you see it. I've put in bidets and cable, gold taps, peach and maroon towels – the lot. It's posh and the punters love it. You should drop in, Amy – any time, still ten quid a throw to you.

I look at the card and put it in my pocket. Thanks, I say, almost in a sad way, Only I've got a boyfriend just now.

She laughs, slightly put out. What about the husband?

I still have him.

You're giving it away in two places –

I know, I say, I know.

I tell her I'll give it a bit of thought. She kisses me and I smell onion and flyspray. As she walks away, the thick gold rings on her fingers flash in the sun.

Harris went out and Gary and I shared a handful of salted peanuts and then snuggled up on the saggy old sofa and it ended with my pants down and a frantic fuck. I wished that Megan wouldn't wait for the give-away noise and then sidle over sneezing, tail beating congratulations. It seemed dirty, having a dog involved.

Shoo! I told her, Go away. Bad dog.

Ah, said Gary, looking to see if there were any crisps left, Poor dog.

Horrible dog. I'm going to stop bringing her, I said, I've had enough.

What would your husband think?

I don't give a fuck what he thinks.

You're leaving him anyway, said Gary seriously, tucking the white tail of his penis into his pants.

But he said it like it was something we'd told some-one to get out of something – and now we were stuck with it.

One evening, he took both my hands in his big ones and said, Listen Amy, I shouldn't say this: I've tried to tell you, but I don't think it's sunk in.

What hasn't?

Harris – he's a liar. Don't believe a thing he tells you. Please Amy, I'm asking you, don't believe anything he tells you about me.

He hasn't told me anything for a while, I said.

Good. Don't trust him, then – if he asks you to do things.

What things? I said. I don't understand.

You can't understand – there's no point – it's not something I can go into now. It's separate from this – I know what you think – just, please Amy, you need to know this. He's not what you think he is.

I laughed. It sounded like one of those films. What do you mean, not what I think? What do I think he is?

You like him, you care for him, I know you do –

I said nothing, because Gary was right, I cared for Harris.

I've told you. He makes up stories. He got us together for a game and now I think he'd like to split us. He's playing. For instance, he told me he kissed you –

I stared, suddenly scared. Gary reached out, curled his fingers right around my wrist. Don't worry, I know him. I know what he's up to. I just thought you should know. Just take care, OK?

Oh, I said, pulling my hand from his, Oh God, I don't know what to think.

It's OK, Amy, he said.

Why don't you just leave? I asked him, because it didn't make sense, all the mystery and Gary hanging on there like some big kid.

Leave this house? – his face was as if he'd never thought of it.

Sure, I nodded, Leave this house. People do it every day.

Gary sighed. It's not that simple.

What are you scared of? What power does he have over you?

Gary hesitated. Less and less, he said. He has less and less and the more he discovers it, the more he's –

What? He's what?

Dangerous. In a way.

I don't understand, I said, What can happen? Who's he going to hurt?

Gary stopped. He took my face between his hands and kissed it. Leave your husband, he said.

What? And live with you and Harris?

No, he said, kissing me again. Alone with me. I'll leave Harris – you're right, I'll go.

He thought about it for a moment and then he added, I never expected all of this, you know.

But Harris and Gary were close as two peas. Sometimes they ignored me, deep in some private joke, some plan, some all-absorbing set of facts. Sometimes I didn't know what I was to them, where I fitted.

One day I heard Harris say to Gary in a low voice, She doesn't go to the Garden any more.

What's that? I said, and he turned to me.

I said you don't go to the Garden any more, do you? It's stopped. We are your adventure now.

Shut up, Harris, Gary said, as if this was part of something they'd already talked about. Leave her alone.

We are enough for her now, Harris said again, smiling. And I have an adventure planned.

What're you saying? I asked him.

Look at her, Harris remarked to Gary. Just like her mother. Nothing scares her. And her beauty. What did I tell you?

Gary stood up and I saw sweat appear on the skin above his lip. Yes, what did you tell me? he said. Go on, tell Amy exactly what you told me.

Harris just sat and smiled – at him, not me.

What? I said.

Nothing, he went.

Amy – Gary began, but I was already walking out of that room, afraid and sick of both of them – their vague, clever games and jumpy logic and invisible rules. Megan jumped up and followed me.

I kept on walking through the hall and out the front door and didn't stop till we were back at the flat.

How was the walk? asked my husband and seeing his dull, accusing face made me turn right around and leave again.

As usual, I had the hunger and was feeling sick and my mouth tasted of tin. He called out after me but I ignored him and continued down the staircase and out again into the bright evening twitter of the road. Megan, stupid animal, tried to follow, but this time I had the satisfaction of shutting the downstairs door in her face.

It was around eight and still light and warm when I got back to Melly Hill – the sound of black-haired men shutting their car boots, women calling down summery gardens, doors slamming, dinners cooking. An ice-cream van had pulled up at the end of the road and shut off its engine, but no one seemed in a hurry to come and buy.

The house looked dozy, sly and fond of itself. I pressed the bell and heard it ting somewhere inside. Then Gary's heavy step at the door.

Amy, he said, and I snapped against him, tight with relief. Maybe he was what I wanted to put in my empty, sicky stomach – his bigness and softness.

Amy, he went again. I said nothing. The hero and heroine on the doorstep.

Stay the night – he was madly kissing my face and wrists.

Gary, of course I can't.

Don't be stupid. You can, you should.

I shouldn't have come back, I said, suddenly tired. I've had enough, if you want to know.

Stay the night, he said.

I smelled the goodness of him – oh, there was so much – and his dark, massive warmth drove me nuts. I can't, I said.

We all sat in the living-room again – a crazy, cock-eyed replay of the hour before – and tears were on my face for no particular reason, except the place I'd come to in my life was baffling me. Harris said he was sorry for what he'd said.

He means it, Gary said.

I'm not your property, I told them, I don't belong to either one of you.

There was silence, as we all took this in. Then Harris said, I've got a little surprise for you, Amy –

I looked up and caught Gary's eye but he quickly looked away. I don't like surprises, I told him.

You'll like this one, Harris told me, and he chucked a packet towards me. So that it fell on the table next to my empty wine glass.

What is it?

Have a look?

I looked inside. Tickets? I said.

Harris hugged himself, leaned over towards me. A present. We're going to Eknos – you and me.

I paused, watching his madly controlling face. I'd never been anywhere. Abroad was the moon to me, my birthplace another world, a time out of a book, unbelievable.

How? I asked him, wondering, How can we possibly go?

It's done, he said, I've booked. We fly on Friday.

127

Don't worry, it's just the weekend. I assume you can get a couple of days off work?

You assume, I said, the panic building in me. You never asked me –

I wanted to surprise you.

I looked at Gary. What about him? I said. Is he coming?

Harris said, Gary has to look after the shop.

I don't want to go without Gary –

Gary doesn't want to come, do you Gary?

I looked at Gary who wouldn't reply, wouldn't look at me. There seemed to be some understanding between them, some power, the thing Gary wouldn't speak of.

Anyway, Gary's not invited. Three days, said Harris, What's the big deal? It's just a trip –

I thought about it. Even with Harris it was tempting. Then I remembered.

I don't even have a passport, I told him, and chucked the tickets back across the table.

You do – he took a reddish passport from his pocket and passed it to me.

Gary took it from my hands, surprised. That's not legal, he said to Harris –

Stay out of this, Harris said without looking at him.

I opened the passport. It had me in it – a murky snap I couldn't remember having had taken. I wondered where he'd got it.

Thanks, I said, trying to hand it back to Harris who wouldn't take it, But I'm not going.

He rose, stiff and cross, agitated. You don't want to see where you were born?

I do, I said, But not now and not without Gary.

Scared? he asked me, and his face looked how it had looked when I'd kissed him – full of anger and disgust.

What would I be scared of?

They both said nothing.

Harris said again, It was a surprise. I wanted to surprise you –

You're always surprising me, I said.

She doesn't like surprises, Gary whispered, smoothing out my fingers, one by one, as if it was his secret, private job to arrange them.

Anyway, what about my husband? I said, suddenly remembering. I couldn't just go off like that without him.

Harris laughed as if that was the biggest joke which maybe it was. It's not that, he said.

OK, I said, It's not that. It's this. I don't feel like it. Gary and I are having a baby and I want to be with him. I'm pregnant, you see.

The moment is good, but nothing like as good as I've imagined it. All sound is sucked from the room and all we're left with is the soft, red exploding of the fire. My cheeks and thighs are hot with the shock of telling.

Gary drops my hand. What?

You heard me.

You're pregnant?

That's right.

Harris doesn't like surprises either. I can tell because of how he's smiling – in a calm, tight, difficult way. At the floor, then at the air, sparks flying out, hard to know what will come next.

Well, well, he says. Well, well.

Maybe we can go to Eknos next summer, I say, With the baby.

Harris comes over to Gary. Congratulations, he goes, You're going to be a father. I bet that comes as a bit of a shock, doesn't it? I bet it's the last thing you thought – ?

129

Gary looks at me and says nothing. I know him. He can't lie. He looks so upset. He moves towards me and then stops himself. Harris smiles, gets up, leaves the room. The door bangs.

Gary sat with his head resting on his hands.
Why didn't you tell me first?
I'm sorry. I was going to. I'm sorry.
He doesn't own us.
Doesn't he?
Gary ignored me, touched the tip of one of my fingers. It's good, he said, It's just – well – incredibly wonderful.
You don't have to say that.
I know I don't have to. I think it's wonderful.
We never said we loved each other.
Yes, we did, he said – forgetting that I never had.
Maybe I should just have an abortion?
Jesus, he looked at me. You've had that thought?
I shrugged. Of course I've had it.
But?
I've thought about it, OK?
Jesus, he said again.
He put his head in his hands. There was a long, long time with neither of us saying anything and I heard the wetness in his mouth.

He sighed again. He got up, sighing like an old man, and saw that the fire was dying down and he started rummaging about in the embers with a stick. Little bits of white drifted up in the air, dissolved against each other. There was the hard snap of wood catching. Smoke. I looked at him. His trousers were shiny where his fatness had made the material wear out.
It's summer, I remarked pointlessly, We really don't need that fire, any more. Why does Harris make us do so many strange things?

He put down the stick, came over and fastened his arms around me. I smelled his sweat.

Harris is always cold, he said. Come here.

I am here.

His lips were on my ear and I felt all my hairs rise to his touch. I can't believe it, he said. How long have you known?

Not long. A few weeks.

A few weeks. Jesus, are you OK?

I'm fine. I've been getting used to it, I told him.

You've been sick?

A little. It's passing now.

When –?

November, I told him.

He moved his hands up and down my back. I'm glad, he said, You've got to understand – I'm just in awe.

He broke off suddenly. You see? he said, Harris was trying to take you away. Now he's going to be angry.

Does it matter? I said impatiently. Forget Harris for a moment. What's he got to do with anything?

But Gary was frowning, stroppy-faced like a kid.

I don't understand you, I said, sitting down.

He relaxed next to me then and the sofa sagged where his big body was.

It's very hard, he said, I want to be straight with you –

Then do it – be straight with me.

I'm frightened you'll hate me. I'm a bad person, Amy. You don't want a bad person for the father of your child –

I felt tears coming into my eyes. We're all bad people, I said, We've all done things. But I'm changing. I'm coming out of it, and I trusted you –

Oh God, said Gary, Don't cry, Amy. You'll make me cry too. I love you –

The door opened and Harris came back in, carrying a bottle and some glasses.

131

It should be champagne, he said.

Gary said, We'll get some tomorrow. Celebrate properly. Is it OK? He turned to me. I mean, can you drink?

I didn't answer or look at him. I took the glass from Harris's hand.

That's my girl, he said, and he kissed me a dry kiss on the cheek.

We all three stood there as the birds called down the lawn and the fire crunched and died. We looked at each other and I don't know what we saw. Then we drank to the bean-sized life-form inside me.

And afterwards there didn't seem much point in going back to my husband and his judgemental dog so, for the first time ever, I spent all the hours of the night in Gary's big wooden bed, in a room where the walls and wardrobe loomed hard and tall out of the half-hearted summer darkness.

I admit it, I've had to keep things from you, Gary said as he stood, smooth and naked, in front of me. All that's going to change, I promise. We have to get away from Harris.

How? I asked him, not believing this could happen. When?

Soon.

When is soon?

As soon as I've spoken to him.

Jesus! I began again, but he closed my mouth with a kiss and I felt his balls brush my thigh.

I love you, I told him, and heard the words buzzing up strangely from where they'd been stored in my heart.

You can't, said Gary, I'm not lovable.

I do –

You can't.

132

But a few minutes later, he said, I'm having you all night – kissing me in a slow rhythm in-between the words – all night, all to myself.

Gary had funny tastes – the free tastes of educated people who get a kick out of shabby, discarded things. I never had a dirty or used-looking thing in my life if I could help it, but Gary collected the things you see in charity shops – old bashed-up trunks and dusty record players and tennis rackets with the guts curling out of them. The room was old and heavy, needing a good lick of paint, and the dust seemed to relish being there.

By his bed was a low chest of drawers painted – by him I reckoned – in bright blue gloss paint and on it was a pile of books, a pack of toothpicks, some chocolate biscuits, a coffee-stained postcard of Groucho Marx and a small golden picture of the Virgin Mary painted on wood.

What's this? I asked him, picking it up.

That? he said. Oh, nothing. An icon.

I stared at it. The Virgin's face was dark and bland and open as a man's face. It reminded me of something, but I couldn't think what.

I didn't know you were religious? I said.

Oh well, you know, he said.

Are you?

No. Not really.

Where's it from?

Somewhere, I don't remember. I think I picked it up abroad.

You only think? You don't know?

He said nothing, touched my cheek with warm fingers.

It looks Greek, I said, though I didn't know why I said that, with my little knowledge.

Maybe, he said, Yes, maybe it's Greek.

He padded next door to the bathroom.

Why do you live here with him? I ask as I pull off my clothes. You've never really told me.

His room is next to the tank or the pipes or something – sounds like we're underwater, bubbles banging against the thin walls.

He helped me out – you know he did.

You sound like a child, I tell him, When you say that.

He smiles. I'm going to have a child.

We'll see, I say, as if to a child.

Your breasts have grown, he says.

Oh well – I sneak a look, weigh their hotness in my hottish hands – maybe.

His bed is piled with blankets – the soft, hairy blankets and cotton sheets of a fat man's bed. I lie there kicking them off as he cleans his teeth and spits and flushes the toilet. When he gets in, everything sighs under him, I roll down the slope and he moves his hands slowly over my body like he's checking its ups and downs and its parts.

Don't stop, I whisper as his head dips and then, Who are you Gary? I hear myself asking him before I know I'm going to ask it.

He doesn't answer. I know he won't answer.

Slow down, he says and pushes me flat against the bed. Open your legs, he says in a low voice and as I do my mouth hushes with hope and desire.

At first, nothing happens, then my body catches light and shoots feelings of sex around itself. I try to keep looking, because looking at what he's doing helps me – but in the end I give in to the pleasure and lie back.

If I bring my knees together it increases the zing – tricks you discover. He leans forward over the bed, puts his mouth up by my ear, kisses my cheek, brow, lobe.

I'm going to stick some fingers in you, he says.

No, I go, snapping shut my legs, wanting it.

He prises them open and he sticks a bunch of fingers into me, a hardness which shoots up and down and makes me open wider, rigid.

He breathes harder. You like that, don't you? he says, I'm going to do it again now.

I can't speak, I shake my head.

OK? he says.

OK, I whisper.

Are you excited?

Mmm, I say.

Say it. Say it excites you.

It excites me.

Then he gets on top and pushes into me and I feel how he's made everything as he likes it, how he's made it as I like it, too. Rough, red pleasure.

We come exactly together, as they do in books.

At work, I finally tell them – I must or else it will tell itself before too long.

So now there's this thread of interest unravelling around the kitchen, and them all crowding round and their greedy eyes all on my stomach – my stomach which actually still fits into my jeans just fine despite the tightness of the zip – all of them looking for signs. And they say they guessed – they knew before I did. And they say: How're you feeling? and Do you know what sex? and Have you thought about names? and I say, I haven't, not yet, because I'm superstitious about these things.

Quite right, they say, nodding.

My husband's child, they all think it is and of course I don't say any different.

So, is he pleased? Paula asks me later, catching me by the ice machine, winding a tea towel around and around her jagged, food-stained fingers.

Kind of, I go, rolling my eyes to show there's more to it than that and she laughs because that small uncertainty is just what she hoped to hear.

It was hot and my husband was away on a conference. I had to go home between shifts to feed Megan and take her up the road to do her business.

Gary came with me – his big body odd and shy, skirting the edges of our empty, familiar rooms. This is where Amy lives, he told himself out loud.

Sit, I said and I pulled him out a chair and scooped dog meat into a metal bowl, a handful of biscuits, fresh water for Megan to drink. He said he preferred to stand.

Come, I said, when I'd finished and wiped my hands, I'll give you a tour – and I showed him the map of my married life – the small, mean rooms with their wall-to-wall beige carpets and the fixings and hooks with our coats on, my husband's and mine – and then on across the wide hall into our bedroom.

Our room, I said.

It's all – very –

I waited for him to say what it was. Very what?

Very inhibiting.

Is it? Why?

You know why, he said.

There was nearly an hour before I had to be back in town, hoovering under the tables and shelling peas – and Megan still had to be taken out. Quickly I pushed Gary back on the bed – my smooth marriage bed – and undid his fly.

He asked me when I was leaving my husband and I said I couldn't leave while he was away because who would feed the dog?

That dog's been the excuse for everything, he said. You couldn't manage without that fucking dog –

I stopped my groping at his fly and looked across the hall where Megan was whimpering and nosing the kitchen door. I wondered whether it was true, that she was an excuse.

And Harris is your excuse, I told him. Maybe we'll both be different when we've got a child –

He moaned as I took his penis out and flipped its soft but slowly hardening end. And I tasted its rim with my tongue, grasped him firmly and lovingly kissed the slit at the end, where the little bead of wet was already oozing out.

Later, we sat together on a sticky bench outside The Star on Alcot Street and I sipped at a lager and lime, him a Grolsch as well as a bag of Scampi Fries.

I'm telling him, I said. It had come to me that there was no other way forward.

I want to be there, he said quickly.

No, I said. That would be a bad move I think.

Oh well, he sighed and took my hand, relieved.

We wandered home along the quiet old streets, up past the Crescent towards the dark, lush slope of Melly Hill. He pulled me into a deserted driveway and slid his hands up under my T-shirt. The skin on my back goosepimpled – not because his fingers were cold, but because they were his.

He undid my bra from behind and then pushed his thumbs up under my arms where there was stubble mixed with Arrid Extra Dry which would leave whiteness on his thumbs.

So, he said.

So, I said.

And he kissed my lips and I put my arms round his neck and kissed him back. After he'd touched my tits a bit more I made him fasten up my bra. He took too long and even then he'd done it on the wrong hook and it was too loose. I told him and he did it up again.

What're you thinking now? he asked me and I admitted I was wondering if my nipples would go dark and squared-off and stick out like in the picture in *Mother* magazine, and he laughed.

He kissed my mouth till it blurred into the rest of me. He licked me, touched the shivery metal of my fillings with the hard tip of his tongue. He held the lobes of my ears and kissed my mouth and I let him till it felt mashed with pleasure.

One last fling, for pocket money.

Mara's new place is neat. Shaggy-carpeted all over and sauna hot, with cheese plants, mirrors, louvred doors – the lot. I admire it out loud.

I haven't topped up my account in ages and now and then I remind myself I've given up. But Steve isn't some unknown punter or casual pick-up. He's an old client of Mara's, tried and trusted.

He doesn't even want oral, says Mara, Just a spot of massage and hand relief. He comes quickly. Eighty quid, no bother, no catches.

It's tempting, I tell her.

Who's to know? she says. He's a doctor – nice bloke.

A doctor?

No, no, she says quickly, None of that.

Because everyone knows that doctors are the worst for wanting to do things to you. Inflict pain. Maybe they know too much about the workings of a woman's body and a straight suck or fuck seems too tame. Maybe it's all that care and curing – making them go wild when they get it on with a girl.

I'm not getting my things off, I tell her.

No, no, she says again, Not at all. I promise you. Hand relief and he only wants it safe. If you're lucky, his beeper might go off before you're through.

Steve's an edgy, narrow-faced man with greying hair that fluffs out over his ears, and the shining eyes of a punished child.

He cracks a joke as I undress him, as I insist on washing that knot of greying flesh and hair with the hand-held shower. Then I lead him to the table and drive those good, strong strokes into his dull, white back and floppy behind.

I can tell by his movements that he wants me to press my fingers in between his buttocks, near his arse, but I don't. I can't stand to go near that spooky place. I end with a gentle, flicking touch over the genitals – Korean they call it – an easy extra which always makes them groan and twitch, the buttocks bunching and hollowing with tension.

How's that, Steve? I go, knowing he will not speak. I watch his fingers knead the towel – the skin around the nails sore and bitten, the black hairs sprouting up to the thickish knuckles.

I know he'll be erect by the time I turn him over.

Ahhh, he goes, as I roll the condom down over him, and I don't snigger, though his face looks funny to me, the eyes rolling up to their whites even with me, a stranger. There's sweat on the shiny curve of his fore-head where, supposedly, the hair used to grow.

I circle his stiff, smallish, rubber-covered penis with my fingers and lean close so he can see my breasts pressing together in my shirt which I've undone to the fourth button. His eyelids flicker and strain, his head tilts. I know he's looking.

He moans, shuts his eyes and turns his head to one side and that's when I burst out laughing.

His eyes flick open.

Sorry, I say, I just thought of something.

He closes them again and I continue, but the wave bursts through and I have to let go I'm laughing so much.

He's irritated. Is it something I'm doing?

No, I say, wiping tears with the heel of my hand, It's me. I just thought about what I'm doing.

He says nothing and I take care to swivel my fingers as I speak, gently lapping the rim of his prick where it's dark with blood and hotness.

He gasps and is about to come and then I do the unforgivable, I drop his prick like a hot sausage.

He cries out, snarls for me to take it again, but already I'm moving away and saying no, I can't do it, I can't bear to see it happen – and I'm out of there before the rubber can even begin to bulge with his juices.

I left the money and Mara told me never to come back, but I felt happier than I'd ever felt in my life. I caught a bus home to tell my husband our life together was over.

I timed it well. He'd just got back from his trip and was sitting in the kitchen with a can of Coke, his tie hotly loosened, arms sticking hairily out of a short-sleeved shirt. I hated those shirts. It helped to have him wearing one whilst I made my speech.

I'm going, I said in a shaky voice, I'm leaving. There's someone else I want to live with.

He looked at me and then he laughed. He laughed and ran his thumb around the sharp metal hole in the can.

I knew you were going to say that, he said. I've been waiting for you to come and say it. I've been seeing someone too as a matter of fact.

I sat down. For how long?

How long what?

140

How long have you been seeing someone?

Does it matter? How long've we been married? I forget, but it seems a fuck of a long time already.

He swigged his drink and looked at me. I couldn't tell what he was thinking.

Do I know her? – I knew it was the wrong thing to ask, but I had to.

I don't think so.

What's her name?

None of your business. But she's thinner than you.

Mine isn't, I said. I'm leaving you for a much fatter man.

I enjoyed his face as he took this in.

I told him about the child.

How do you know it isn't mine? he said immediately, because all men always think their particular seed's the most potent.

Because you and me took – precautions, I said.

And with him?

We didn't. Don't worry, I said, It's not yours.

He stared at the floor. A little line zig-zagged under his eyes. All this time, he said, And I went down on my knees and begged you and you wouldn't start a family.

I know, I said and felt my whole body shiver. I know.

Gary and I stood still in the park and watched the buggies rolling through the yellowish grass and the dust.

Each child had on a sunhat and carried a bottle of juice or a little carton with a straw. Some had bare feet and some had gingham canvas sandals that showed their toes.

The parents pushed with blank, dazed faces, the women with dark streaks under their eyes and the men with lit cigarettes between their lips, looking away at every opportunity, seeking escape in the dull, hot shadows under the trees.

He piled all my stuff up on the landing outside our front door and I went with Gary in the shop's van to collect it. It wasn't till then that I realised it was nothing, all this clobber that I had, that I thought I couldn't live without. Just clothes, tapes and a rocking chair. A couple of plants, a lampshade for which my husband childishly insisted on keeping the base. It no longer looked like mine. In Melly Hill it would dissolve to nothing.

He stayed in the living-room while Gary and I carried it all downstairs, so he didn't have to set eyes on Gary. When we were done, I knocked on the door and called out a supposedly friendly goodbye but he didn't reply and all I could hear was the radio playing and a tap running.

So you're leaving your husband, Harris said, For the fat man?

I love Gary, I told him.

I know you do, he said, But it's a shock. It's not what I would have predicted –

I know that, I said, but I still felt like the kitten to his piece of string. What would you have predicted, then?

He hesitated, looked at me. You're forgetting, he said, It was my idea. I asked you to see him in the first place.

I'm not forgetting at all, I told him. You said he needed a girlfriend –

But not a fucking family.

Harris took my hand and kissed my fingers. It suits you, he said, You're looking more like you and less like her.

Her?

142

Less like Jody. Less like your mother.

And something shifted as he spoke, a blackness dissolved and I saw something, just for a second, which made my heart jump.

You didn't like her, did you? I said.

He did not look at me.

What is it? I asked him. What were you predicting, what were you hoping to do?

Do?

I know you're just renting this house. I know you came here to look for me –

He stood up and I knew he wouldn't deny it. He was calm.

Who told you that?

No one told me, I said, suddenly not liking the look on his face. I found it out.

He considered this and then he sighed.

Promise me one thing, Amy, he said, Don't go off and leave me. Don't you and Gary go. I like babies. I want to help. Let me be your family. It's not just Gary, you know, it's me – I need a family too.

I sat there as confused as when I'd first met him. I felt the baby celebrating – dancing on my heart.

Seven

Jimmy was the name we gave our baby – and when people tried to put us right, saying – Oh, so you're calling him James – we narrowed our eyes and said, No, no, not James, just Jimmy.

For they weren't the same at all, the long and the short of that name, and why should we have both if we didn't want them? We were parents now. We could do what we liked. Gary said no one could stop us naming our child Mr Blue Lagoon if we fancied it. Here was something that was ours, made from scratch just by us, no one else's business, thank you.

Our own child. I whispered it to myself as I sat on the toilet or closed my eyes to sleep. Sometimes I tried the words out aloud to Gary and got a kick out of seeing his face shimmy to attention.

Nobody is normal when it comes to babies. Just because other people have done it and survived, doesn't mean you will. Jimmy's birth was almost an operation, and all because my uterus was such a special, complicated shape.

Heart-shaped, the doctor said, curling four of his fingers to demonstrate. Odds are your mother's was the same.

I don't care about the odds, I said as the pain closed over my head, Get this fucking baby out of me.

Everywhere there were machines, red lights. I walked up and down that humming room. They'd stuck a

crochet hook up my cunt, twiddled it a bit, and now
there was a slow hotness as my waters leaked out. The
sanitary pad they gave me was big and fat as a nappy
and covered in fine webbing like a string vest and had
a loop at either end.

For the belt, the nurse said.

Gary stared, fascinated, but I wasn't having any belt.
I kept mine in place by clenching my thighs and
shoving it back every time it rode up in my pants.

Sometimes I had to lie back while they put on gloves
and moved their rubber fingers inside me and it hurt
a bit but not too much, especially when you considered
all the other things I'd had up there.

A heart-shaped uterus. Pretty romantic, huh? Gary
congratulated me from his slump in the rocking chair.

A half-eaten chicken salad roll was on his lap and
when he came over and touched my face, his fingers
smelled of granary baps and sweet, crunchy leaves.

You think it's never going to happen, that you'll walk
around forever with your bump and your pad between
your legs. But five hours later my pants are off, my
belly's shrunk, and my own baby's cries are exploding
in my ears.

I'm sweating and shaking and there are blood
splashes between my legs and over the floor and what
I'm having trouble believing is that this noise is anything to do with me – this baby crying noise that's
come right out of me – one minute lodged silently in
my cunt, the next stretching me wide, then slipping
between my thighs and brashly out into the world.

I sit back and hold it in my arms, wrapped in its stiff
hospital sheet, letters and numbers stamped in pale
purple, the fabric puckered around the small, brightly
furious face.

How is it? I whisper.

146

The midwife laughs. It's fine and it's male.

Fuck me, whispers Gary, We did it. We made a real, live beautiful boy!

Our boy. I never thought I'd be so happy, having a baby, but now I know it's everything, the day to day, the coming and going, the life that I've been waiting for.

Those first moments of his, we shut out the world and just have our own two bodies bare under the sheets – his dampness sweet and silky against mine. And he looks at me with those sharp, curranty eyes and I look at him and from now on I know this is the way it will be. I press my tit into his mouth and he spits it back. Then finds it, half sucks, stops and blinks.

Love is a stain, spreading before you can stop it.

Jimmy was already two days old when Harris shuffled into the ward and sat on a PVC chair the mustardy colour of baby shit.

I'd forgotten him already, with Jimmy and every-thing. He looked like nothing I knew – like a person in a movie or the friend of a friend. His eyes reminded me of photos of nature – of craggy birds of prey. His linen jacket was as creased as ever, the lining hanging out, ripped at the bottom. He was unshaven and his bootlaces flapped, half undone.

Hello, stranger, I said.

Amy, love – he raised a hand – It's boiling in here.

I shrugged.

How are you? he said as if someone had been re-hearsing him on what to say.

Well, Harris, to tell you the truth. I'm on holiday.

It was true, I was loving it, enjoying myself, all tucked up with Jimmy in the dullish warmth. It was only a couple of nights, but I was well settled at this mother and baby hotel.

You lay back and did nothing. Your biggest exercise was the walk to the bathroom. You ticked a card and the meals were brought to you – neat lumps of things in pretty colours and tasting of nothing – and afterwards you could listen to music on the radio headphones while you fed and gazed at your perfect and startling child.

There was a library for reading, and a chapel for praying and kiosks to buy magazines and sandwiches and even outsize clothes and stuff. There was a shop selling red and lurid turquoise carnations and metallic balloons on a stick and the lights stayed glowing all night, as if the hospital had its own climate and twilight and dawn.

The girl who brought the tea round was called Lucia and she was chatty. She told me she had a sister who was a makeup artist – specialising in brides on the big day. When I told her I wasn't even married to little Jimmy's father (naturally I left my husband out of the picture), she laughed and said did I know that six out of ten of the brides her sister did split up within the first five years, anyway? I said it didn't surprise me. Maybe she doesn't make them attractive enough, I said.

This she found funny. She laughed till she spilt the tea. I'll tell her that, she said.

Harris went off in a corner and nattered to Gary. I didn't mind. I felt like the Queen. I felt that for once the world couldn't get moving without me, so I wasn't in danger of missing anything. Wrong on both counts.

I noticed how nervous Harris was, picking away at the rough skin on his thumbs, flicking glances here and there. He barely took in the babe or me. Some men are scared when you get milk in your tits and Harris – though sometimes I forgot it – was an old man and they are the scaredest.

After ten minutes, he did come over, nudged Jimmy's curled fist bud with the end of his finger.

Hello, he said to Jimmy and waited like it was possible he might reply.

Harris said he could see traces of my brother and I looked carefully. It had never come into my mind to look for Paul.

He nodded. Same hair, same strange eyes.

All babies have those eyes, I told him, because I did not want him to be in charge of how Jimmy looked or which blend of people was supposed to be in him.

The hospital wasn't like the hygienic American ones you see on the TV. Paint was peeling, the toilets smelled of paper and plastic and piss and you didn't know how many times people'd died in your bed or how.

Much as I liked being waited on, after three days the noise of other people getting no sleep, and all those labour stories the same but different, was getting to me and I was ready to go. I told Gary this as he made a show of not dozing in the rocking-chair.

He jumped and opened his eyes. Don't worry, he said, We'll get you out – and he heaved himself up and wandered off to find I don't know who.

I stared after him, his bigness going further and further away from me across the ward, and I tried to see him as others saw him but I couldn't trick myself into doing it. So who was he? That was always the trouble with Gary – it was like I'd never had any perspective on him, never been anywhere but slap bang right close up.

In my childhood, Eileen (who based the whole point of her life on crippled things) adopted a feral cat – wired and wiry, scalp bald in patches and flecked with blackish blood. It yowled for love, but you also knew

149

that it would gladly give you a rollercoaster ride on its teeth if you were any smaller.

Now Jimmy has made me into that cat, a feral thing, claws drawn. I smell dangers I couldn't smell before. I am unfazed by blood. I would wait on a stair, heartbeat suffocating, a meat knife wrapped sharply under my coat, ready for the kill. I would do anything to keep Jimmy safe – to keep him alive and breathing and mine.

Eventually the cat went under the wheels of a lorry, chasing shadows. Eileen grieved, but Brian said thank God he was saved the cost of getting it put down.

Gary was so proud. He couldn't care less who Jimmy looked like. All he could see was everything he'd hoped for coming true.

Left to himself, he'd never have gone back to work. He was one of those fathers you read about, who carry dribble cloths and wet wipes around and wait at the school gates and don't get bored pushing a crowd of children on the swings.

He talked to Jimmy, told him jokes and kissed his nose and picked him up and diddled him around in his arms. He looked into his eyes and told him to his face how handsome and perfect and clever he was. He made Disney noises to try catch his first smile, his first laugh. He opened up the small, tight fists and fished out all the grit and fluff that got trapped sweatily in them.

He put batches of kisses on the pimply chin, where a dribble of see-through milk escaped from blueish lips. He could sit patiently and watch the bubbles Jimmy blew in his sleep, the snuffles, the invisible ins and outs of his breath. He could walk Jimmy up and down the room, push the pram back and forwards with his foot without getting a cramp, crash out in front of the TV with the kid cradled snug in the crook of his arm.

He was the best father.

He left for the shop late and came home early. He bought little gifts home for me: a pair of spirally earrings, silken slices of parma ham, an enamelled egg, a book of American love poems full of 'if this' and 'if that'. I wore the earrings even though they kept on catching on Jimmy's shawl, ate the ham, and put the egg and the poems on the mantelpiece among the other things he'd bought me.

He didn't complain about changing nappies. He cleaned Jimmy's cord stump and tipped the special powder into it. He did shopping and cooked me food and sang me to sleep. He grew an extra few hairs on his chest where previously there'd been hardly any and we laughed about this as we undressed each other.

At night, he sometimes sat up late and talked to Harris. I don't know what they talked about and I couldn't care. Sometimes I thought I heard them shouting, but I slept and my sleeps were all the same, a sudden drop into darkness. I had no dreams. I saw at last why they called it falling.

Jimmy was going easily for four hours between feeds and I thought it was good of Harris to offer to mind him while I went to the shops. I needed a walk, a rest, the aloneness.

When I got back, Jimmy was asleep and Harris was reading the paper. I thanked him. No trouble, he said, handing me Jimmy's extra dummy in its see-through case, Any time.

But Gary was furious when he came home and heard about it. Don't you ever do that again, he told me, as I sat on our bed changing Jimmy, wiping his bum down with pink lotion. He's not to be trusted. I don't want him left alone with our child. Don't you understand, Amy?

What could happen? I asked him calmly, as I smeared Drapolene all over Jimmy's soft behind.

Gary's belly shook when he was angry. He stood at the window and you could see the red mark his jeans belt had made in his flesh. I don't even want to think about it, he said.

Next day he said had I noticed he'd lost weight?

No! I cried straightaway, I don't want you to.

He looked at me, disbelieving, glanced sideways into the mirror and ran his fingers through his sticky-up hair.

I'm not going to be fat all my life.

You're not fat.

Come on, Amy. He sat down, put his head in his hands and looked as if he was thinking of something else to say. Then he just sighed – I am.

I said nothing. I didn't know how to disagree in a way that would make him take notice.

I don't want my son to see me fat.

Jimmy was asleep in my arms. I disengaged my slippery teat from his mouth and laid him on the bed in his shawl. I was used to handling him now. You could tell he was my baby, by the way I seemed to do things without thinking. If I'd been able to look in on myself, I'd have been impressed. I was genuinely motherly.

It's never worried you before, I pointed out.

How do you know what worries me? he said. You don't know anything, Amy. You think you do, but you don't.

It's Harris, isn't it? I said, because it was always Harris at the root of our troubles.

You want to spend your life under his roof? Gary said, Is that what you want? You're used to a husband and a place of your own. You'll be back at the restaurant in a month, full pay. We can get somewhere. We're a

152

family. Even a rented place would be better than this.

I stared into space. Jimmy gave a little snuffle and then a cough.

I wouldn't want to hurt him, I said slowly.

The child sleeps between us in our big, saggy bed on a piece of enchanted sheepskin that seems to eat up his vomit and piss and hardly needs washing. Gary says he wonders why everyone doesn't sleep on one, then you wouldn't have to bother with changing the sheets half so often. But, bearing in mind what we get up to, I reckon you'd still be better off changing them.

Sometimes when I'm lying on my side feeding Jimmy, Gary comes up behind and starts stroking my bottom and my thighs and the hot, hairy baby hole which still pours blood on to a pad.

Sometimes he puts his whole finger into the hole – Does that feel good? he'll say softly, breath humming in my ear. But he doesn't need an answer, I'm squirming and sighing so much. He doesn't mind the blood. He doesn't mind any bit of me. He'll taste any part of my body with his mouth, whatever's coming out.

He strokes all around the hole while I'm wriggling, my nipple still in Jimmy. If it comes out mid-feed, we get a big fuss, so I take care not to move around too much. And sometimes Gary takes his finger out and licks it and puts it back in again, moving upwards and backwards, flicking around till my breath falls away in little spills and bursts. All while Jimmy's sucking, enjoying a nice long meal.

Afterwards, we lay him in the crib by the bed and Gary enters me so gently it feels like warm dough sliding in and rising. At first I worry that my stitches will hurt or even break, but just as Gary gets big for me, so I can grow for him and we fit together as we always did.

153

There, he sighs, Can you feel that?

He tries sucking my nipples but the unreal sweetness of my milk puts him off. I point out that I've swallowed his bitter milk, but he laughs and says it's not the same. This milk is Jimmy's he says, It's made for Jimmy.

Oh, and who is yours made for?

For you.

The first orgasm after the birth sends me to heaven and back – I'm not joking – electric light bulbs snapping in my head, hot lines down my limbs, a magnet drawing my cunt to the centre of the earth. Gary laughs when I put it like this, but to me there's no other way.

We should have babies more often, he says.

When we've finished, he wipes the blood off his cock with an old towel and we take Jimmy back in-between us.

It's a shame about the crib. It was given us by the restaurant – expensive carved cherrywood with a Sleeping Beauty sconce – and it only gets used when we fuck.

Having a baby jogs your memory – flashes of yourself are delivered back to you, bits you'd forgotten laid out like old clothes on the bed.

When they brought my mother's body out of the sea, she smelt bad, because it had been a few days. I made myself invisible on the sand, but a man I knew came up to me and said, Don't cry, I'll make you feel better.

I knew the man so it was safe and I was too young not to play games. When he threw me up in the air, I laughed and laughed, loving the feel of it in my stomach, the up and down you couldn't stop, the falling squeeze in my chest.

But then it changed and I was scared, like when tickling moves out of fun and into pissing and pain. I

154

tried to shout for him to stop, but I couldn't get the breath for even that small word, and my tears were falling.

He threw me so hard I was sick right there on the sand.

Sometimes it's like you're attached to your new baby by a thread – not an invisible one, but a strong, hard, dragging line so visible to the world that you daren't break it even for a second in case you're thought a bad mother. Forget reading a magazine or doing your face or moving from room to room like a free person. You can't even go to the toilet without a hurry-up and a secret, snarling guilt.

When he's full of milk and swallowed at last by sleep, you creep away, but the actual doing of it tugs that thread and rouses him. Without looking, his black eyes can find you in the room. And your body's begging you to take a bath, to change your pants so stiff with blood that it's pulling at your hairs down there, to relax and think your own thoughts for a moment. So what you do is, you place him in his basket right next to you on the bath mat and step into the full bath. A moment of swimmy silence, but then he starts up – a sneezy, hesitant sound at first, then the little fists flailing, the lips sucking in breath, working up to the full mullarkey.

Gary pops his head around, a mouthful of Mini Wheats and milk. Ignore him, he goes, He'll settle. You enjoy your bath. I'll bring you a cup of tea.

Enjoy? Thin milk springs from my tits and tears run down over my nipples, both liquids falling into the hot, blossomy water.

So my sensitive fat man puts down the cereal bowl and lays a hand on my head, passes me some bunched-up toilet paper, but the wetness of my weeping fingers dissolves it and it clings so I have to dunk my hand in the bath and now everything's mixed up, floating.

I'll take him, he says. And as he shoulders our baby, a loud burp escapes. There, says Gary, as if he knows everything there is to know in the world.

As he walks so calmly from the room, something snatches at my heart, whether memory or loss or excitement, it's hard to say.

My husband's solicitor contacted me to say my husband wanted a divorce and quick as possible as he was wanting to get married again.

Fine, I said, But couldn't he have asked me himself?

He said his client would prefer not to be involved. His emotions were still too keenly exposed.

This vision of my husband was new and intriguing to me.

Jimmy was getting on for four months old and cutting a bottom tooth when Gary found us a place of our own.

We'll take it, he said, before I'd even seen it, While we look for something better.

You're that desperate? I said.

He nodded. I don't trust Harris any more. We've moved beyond that.

But – you were such good friends –

Things change. It's over between us, he said sharply. Whatever you'd like to think there was.

It was small, he said – two rooms and a kitchen, toilet, shower – but it was a good walk from Melly Hill and that was the point. He knew the landlady, something to do with the shop. She said she'd waive the deposit. Which makes all the difference, he said.

He asked me if I wanted to see it. I said, what was the point. He'd made up his mind, hadn't he? We were going there anyway.

It's for the best, he said.

He kissed me and you could tell he was distracted by the idea of our new life together because he didn't even manage to finish the kiss.

At the baby clinic, I didn't want to talk to anyone else, even though there was so much chummy lining up of buggies and comparing of size and weight and habits.

I took my number card and I waited on the last of the scuffy, orange plastic chairs.

Jimmy never seemed to put on a lot, but they said he was safely within normal – at a fair enough place on the chart. Last time the woman had done a cross with her pencil in a little square and joined it up with another. I'd leaned over and nodded in an interested way, though I couldn't see how to discover much of my own baby in the light of so much plotting and maths.

Hey now, little man, she said, as she got me to unwrap him and place him on the weighing scales. Hey now, what's all the fuss? Don't you like your momma getting you all bare?

They always said to take the nappy off, though I couldn't see that it weighed anything. It was clean and dry so I folded the tapes over to use it again and, wouldn't you know, as soon as I laid him on the blue paper towel, he pissed – a shaky explosion of yellow, spattering back down on his little, skinny chest and marking her blue file of notes.

Beats me, she said, using a Kleenex to blot her file. Take off the nappy and that's when they get the urge to go. Thought you'd give us a little fountain, eh? she said to Jimmy. Is that what you thought?

Jimmy stared up at her in his nakedness, not quite moved to smile, not quite bothered to cry. I pressed him back into his nappy and suit and did up the poppers and we lined up for the chatting bit.

The health visitor took his gold book and flicked through it. She looked at me carefully and asked if I was getting enough sleep and I said, I don't know. What's enough?

Do you get much help? she said, From your husband?

He does everything, I told her and it was more or less true. Cooking, cleaning, washing, the lot.

She laughed and said could I please send him round to her place rightaway as she could use the help. And what about sex? she said.

What about it? I flushed, wondering if she intended me to think she was short in that department too.

Everything OK? What contraception are you using?

I told her we used Durex and she asked did I need any more? I said I'd happily take some, though the truth was Gary and me had been leaving it mostly to chance, now that our bodies were so merged, now that we were a family. I hadn't given it much thought, but to my mind we were now solid as a rooted tree: whatever wanted to grow off of us could grow and good luck to it.

I take it you wouldn't want to fall pregnant just now? she said, like reading my thoughts – and I laughed and said I hadn't even had a period yet.

Don't let that fool you, she said. Then she asked me about Jimmy moving on to solids.

Does he need it? I said.

Oh, she said, A bit of mashed-up banana, or some baby rice would be OK. Try it. If he's not fussed, leave it another week or so.

Jimmy never seemed fussed about anything except my two, tasty, raw nipples but, when I got him home, I took a ripe banana and attacked it with a fork till it was a yellow pulp and loaded it on to his pale-blue plastic spoon and strapped him into his rocker.

At first he made a terrible face and poked out his tongue and dribbled the whole lot back at me, but I kept going and finally he gave in and gulped it down, really just for something to do.

I saw the whole thing – pulp and a little spill of blackish seeds – come out in his nappy later. It made me sad, 'cause it meant he'd joined the human race: no more of that lovely, pure-yellow, sweet-smelling baby shit.

I am lying next to Jimmy on the bed and faraway someone is digging up the road – the kind of noise that buzzes in your teeth and gums if you get close up.

Things are coming back to me and it's summer and between my breasts I'm sweaty and some bits of black have stuck on my skin. I can smell the good and gunky smell of the glue Gary's used to fix the tiles in the toilet next door.

Jimmy is half asleep, half awake – fussing, opening and closing his fingers – making up his mind whether to bother crying or not. I peer into his face and he smiles at me and the shiny, wet, round end of his tongue appears. I cradle his head where the pulse jumps, kiss him till his honey smell makes me sneeze.

Sometimes I lie and watch my memories like telly: shapes drifting past, some believable and some not.

Just before we left Melly Hill, Harris bought Jimmy a present of a plastic house that you attached with a plastic strap to his cot and you could pull a string and it played 'Pop Goes the Weasel'.

He's too young to pull that, Gary said meanly and straightaway as I unwrapped it. He hasn't got the reflexes yet.

It's great, I told Harris, I'll fix it up and he can look

159

at it. He's really into looking at things now.

Jimmy was fretting when I put him down in the cot, but the moment he saw Harris's house, it was like magic, he just shut up and stared. I put my head down close between the bars and tried to think what he was seeing. The house had its windows and doors arranged in a fairytale way, to give the feeling of a face – a sleepy, droopy, homey face with a thin red mouth that was the door.

Look at him, Harris said, He can't take his eyes off it. I think he likes it.

Of course he does, I said, though I could feel Gary having his mixture of thoughts from the corner of the room.

A few days later, Jimmy learned that he could bash the house with his little fists so it clacked against the bars of his cot. The clacking got so loud that when we wanted to go to sleep, we had to pull it out on to the other side of the bumper so he couldn't reach it.

Once, I woke in the middle of the night to hear 'Pop Goes the Weasel' playing – just a few, winding-down bars – and I ran in to find that – on the other side of the bumper – the string had been pulled just a little tiny bit.

He'll have done it in his sleep, Gary said, There's no other explanation.

I agreed with him. We were both so shattered. Sometimes the easiest reason has to do.

The flat was in Lalla Road, near Chantney Bridge, around the corner, ironically enough, from the Garden for the Blind.

Does it bother you? Gary asked me as if he'd only just thought of it.

It's all there is, I said – scared to imagine I might not be over that part of my life.

The houses were made of that grand, old, blond stone, stained blackish in places where they needed cleaning up. You see them doing it with jets of water – an expensive business.

But this was the uncared-for end. Black sacks of rubbish stood on the pavements. The dried out remains of someone's cat was plastered to the street.

We moved in one hot afternoon when the trees were dusted with pollen, air heady like chocolate. Gary put in his key and once we were in the hall, the darkness and sharp dampness fell around us. The carpet was threadbare, covered in rubbish and papers shoved through the door.

It's in perfectly good nick, he muttered, though I'd said nothing, Just needs a lick of paint here and there.

I carried on saying nothing. Jimmy had a dissolving rusk in his fist and he let it drop so I picked it up and threw it away.

Swirly carpets, Gary said as he led me into the bedroom. I looked around me at our new love nest. It was hard to imagine living within those walls, but then other people's walls – bare and pointless – are always hard to love.

Where will Jimmy sleep?

With us, he said, As before.

And later?

We'll sort something out.

All the furniture was brown and smelled of dogs and oldness.

We stood by the window and looked out on a concrete yard where a rusty child's trike had a pool of rain on the seat.

Jimmy won't have a garden, I said.

We'll make a garden.

I was being a cow. I lit a cigarette, making out that it was the first since Jimmy's birth.

Don't start on at me, I said.

Gary took a breath and said not a word, but he batted smoke away with his hand.

It needs doing up, he said, I know it does.

We waited outside for the van containing what little furniture we possessed. I enjoyed the smoke, it was good to fill myself up with something bad.

It's a fresh start. I want us to be a family, he said, as if it was the first time he'd had the idea.

I'd called Hetty and fixed a date for going back to work and now I had to look around for a minder, but the idea of leaving my Jimmy in someone else's house filled me with dread.

The evening shifts would be fine – I'd only do a couple and Gary would have him – but four-day shifts were required each week. A registered childminder had put a handwritten ad in the newsagent on Chantney Bridge, saying she had a space and references were available etc, etc, and I'd phoned her up and arranged to see her. But her telephone manner was sad and rasping and she never even asked my baby's name.

Sad and rasping? Gary repeated softly as he lay behind me in bed, his warmth getting harder and more distracting as it pressed between my two bare cheeks. I don't get it – how can you know what she's like, just from over the fucking phone?

It's what I'm saying, I told him, my juices already provoked by his poking, I have these feelings. I can't ignore them.

It was the truth. All my life I've known things and my baby was the most certain thing – like a person I'd been expecting, someone I already knew, who would join me one of these days. So when he came out, it wasn't like surprise exactly, but a relief, a recognition

162

– the knowing that ever since I was a small child myself, I'd been waiting for Jimmy, knowing my Jimmy was on his way to me.

I push my baby in his pram in the Garden for the Blind and wonder if you can turn tricks with a kid in tow. I imagine it depends on how good a sleeper he is. Jimmy's not at all bad these days, only waking once in the night and having a good long doze you can rely on after lunch.

He's asleep now – fists raised like a muscle man, head turned perfectly to one side on the pram blanket which has a pattern of pink and blue bunnies chasing. The side of his head he prefers to sleep on has a patch of bald on it, the hair so soft it's worn away.

Only one man is sitting there on the furthest bench. He's youngish, not bad-looking, in a denim shirt and smoking a cigarette and staring at the blue winding path. He says nothing when I come over and sit down too. I look at him and he still says nothing, but I know he's aware. I smile and he makes a show of peering in the pram.

Boy or girl?

A girl, I tell him – thinking, what do you care? Only after one thing – Little Daphne.

Little Daphne? he says.

My mother's name.

Oh, he goes, That's nice, then.

We sit. All the birdies are tweeting and you can hear the dull, faraway moan of the traffic.

I don't suppose you want a cigarette? he says.

Don't I? Why not?

Bad for the babby, isn't it?

I shrug, take one from the offered packet, and he holds the lighter flame steady in front of my eyes.

Lovely day, he says. Come here a lot, do you?

No, I say, But I used to –

Oh yeah?

I used to pick up men here.

He takes a nip of his cigarette and turns his head and I can feel him looking. I look straight ahead. I let him watch the side of my face.

What? he says.

I open my mouth and then shut it. Pick men up, I say. You know. For money.

Silence. He crushes his cigarette under his heel, looking half-sad, half-scared, half-hopeful – they mostly do. I wonder about offering him a blow-job. I wonder about taking him to Mara's and showing him my breasts or undoing his trousers and feeling his little, greedily worried cock spring out.

I thought you were a married lady, he says.

I laugh and look into his face and place a hand on his thigh and then I remove it.

Just remembered something I have to do, I tell him.

See you tomorrow? he goes.

If you say so – I unbrake the pram – Better get him back for his feed.

He doesn't notice little Daphne's had a sex-change. He's watching my arse as it wobbles away over the gravel.

But next day I was too busy painting the kitchen to go bothering men in the Garden for the Blind.

I'd got the emulsion. I was doing it white all over, flat, brilliant white into all the shadows and cracks.

Gary came in with Jimmy while I was doing it and asked if I wanted him to take over, but I said no thanks, I was quite happy. I liked the relaxation of it.

Jimmy had been fretful all morning, trying to feed, but giving up after a few sucks, then crying again with hunger the very next minute. I wondered if it was me, my breasts, and I was getting tempted to try him on a bottle. But when I mentioned the idea to Gary, he said, no – he liked me feeding his son from my body.

He'd been walking up and down with him, but every time he stopped walking, Jimmy started up again. Maybe he really was hungry. Maybe he was going to be a great big beefy lad like his Dad.

Pretty soon Gary had to go into work. I'll take him, if you want, I said, even though I really wanted to go on with the painting.

It's OK, Gary said.

More crying.

I don't want to leave you with this, he said.

Put him down, I told him, Let him cry for a few minutes.

I've tried that, said Gary.

Try for a bit longer. He probably just needs to sleep.

Gary sighed. He just didn't like to let Jimmy cry – it went against all the caring side of his nature.

I put down the paint-brush and wiped my fingers on my shorts. Perhaps he's cutting a tooth, I said.

Already?

I don't know. Maybe. It could be now.

I put my cleanest finger in and felt Jimmy's hot little gum. There was plenty of spit – in fact the spit was spilling over, wetting my hand. But as soon as I touched him, Jimmy began to cry, his mouth wide and dark.

When Gary left for work, I put him in his crib and let him scream for a bit and then, when I couldn't bear it, I picked him up and lay on the bed with him. He carried on and I felt myself wanting to shake him but I didn't want to dislodge a bit of his brain like they do in the papers – you can go to prison for that and rightly so – so I moved away. Then I lay back down and cried with him.

I took his temperature. It was just a fraction under normal.

I had him almost quiet, settling in the crook of my arm, but then I made a mistake and offered him a tit and he took another big breath, building to a cry.

I ran from the room and didn't stop till the sound was muffled by two doors. I waited. My heart was beating. I counted to ten, then twenty, then thirty.

By lunchtime he'd only been quiet for about ten minutes and I had a dragging headache.

I was scared I really was going to harm him if he didn't stop, so I put him in the pram and marched up and down the hall, but you couldn't turn when you got to the end and had to shuffle backwards, moving the Hoover out of the way as you did.

I swept him up in one quick movement out of the pram and carried him back through into the bedroom and dropped him on the bed and yelled at him. He yelled back, his face wet and terrible. Then I phoned Harris.

I'm coming over, he said.

No, I went, because something about it felt wrong. But it was too late and he'd put down the phone and was on his way, so I'd got what I wanted and now I could cry till he got here.

I panicked. A scream was settling silently in my throat – I was suddenly mad with the idea that I mustn't on any account see Harris.

I put Jimmy back in the pram, grabbed my keys and set off, adjusting the sunshade so I couldn't see his face. Shut up, I whispered as he carried on bawling – because Harris would be here in ten minutes flat and the noise would certainly give us away.

We're going on an adventure, little man, I told him chirpily, Just around the block. I tried to put on his sailor sunhat with the elastic under the chin but he kept struggling and pushing it off so in the end I gave up and stuffed it in the changing bag along with the wet wipes and the Pampers.

His little forehead was covered with sweat from crying so much. Tears and sweat were falling into his hair. There was no point in wiping it because more would come.

He screamed for a bit longer and then he fell asleep mid-scream. As the silence burned in my grateful ears, I felt myself relaxing and getting some common sense back. I saw how crazy and stupid I'd been, running away. What was I scared of? What was Harris going to think, coming to help like that and finding no one?

I said something to myself – I don't know what – and turned around and went back. It wasn't far. We'd only got as far as the crossing at the bottom of Lumley Row. I knew he'd be there and he was, waiting on the steps, hands in pockets and smiling to himself all dramatic and expectant, like he'd known we'd just popped out and were coming back. I hushed my fingers to my lips to show that Jimmy was asleep. Even bumping him up the steps didn't wake him.

Panic over, I whispered to him with a little laugh as we got in the hall, I'm sorry I called you. You can go home now.

Without thinking, I felt Jimmy's head. His face was pushed down in the pillow and he seemed to sigh. He felt burning to my touch, but then my hands were unusually cold and shaky.

Is he OK? Harris put his hand on my shoulder and bent stiffly towards the pram.

He's cried himself into a right old sweat, I said like some cheery old mum you see in the park, But he'll live.

Harris won't go.

He makes me a cup of tea and brings it to me in the living-room. I sip it gratefully even though it's too weak and cold and kettle-tasting. I wonder if he even let it come to the boil.

We leave Jimmy sleeping in the hall. Babies can sleep anywhere, everyone knows that. It makes no difference what's going on around them. Once they're off, they're off, thank God.

I thank Harris for the tea anyway and feel my eyes closing.

You sleep, he says in quite a kind voice, I'll sit here. I'll take him out again if he wakes up.

I can hear him flipping open his tin, starting to roll a cigarette.

Do one for me, I say.

No, he goes, You need to rest – and I give in, so relieved to be taken care of and told what to do. Even so, there's a secret thing – a worry, buzzing between my ears, and for a moment I'm about to think something and then I don't. Sometimes you have to resist your thoughts or the world would come to a standstill. It's a sign of being a grown-up.

I'm wondering if he should see the doctor, I say, yawning to push back the tears springing to my eyes.

Why? Harris asks me – and I find I can't think of why.

It's just, I say, trying to sort out the most likely words, It's just that it's been a bad day.

For you?

For both of us.

He's a healthy baby, says Harris, All babies cry. It's what babies do.

And I'm thinking he must be right, it's true, Jimmy's a healthy baby, he's fine and normal. In all his life all he ever had was one brief cold.

*

I wake a short while later and the room is chilly because the sun's gone and so has Harris. The radio is on, very quiet, in the kitchen – careful, explaining voices. He must have left it for me.

I lie for a moment, enjoying the comforting growl of the voices, then remember and jump up to check Jimmy, glad that he's slept so long. The hall is dark and cool and I prise up the sunshade with its wobbly fringe and see the normal small shape of him under the covers. He's still lying in the same position, head turned to the side, away from me.

How I left him.

And then the blood is up in my face, thumping panic behind my eyes, because I know how Jimmy sleeps and this is not it. Something is not there or gone completely wrong – What's wrong, Jimmy? – and now my hand is madly groping to touch his face. His very white, sad face. His face that has not moved.

I press the fattish baby lips with my thumb, feel how they're all slow and don't twitch at my touch – and how his head stays asleep and doesn't move. I pull on his shoulder, put the other hand round to pick him up, but his weight drags through the still air to me, there's no movement, no quick sigh, no sudden startle of arms and legs. My baby's eyes stay stuck closed, his mouth slightly open. A little dribble of sick is on the blanket where his head was.

You think these things can't happen, that normal life will stick safely around you because you're you, not turn you into one of those if-only people you read about who lose their kids.

Trying to stop myself from falling, I bang open the front door and scream for help, then pick up Jimmy, who's now just dangling in his blankets and carry him to the phone, dial the emergency and all the while I'm talking to him. It'll be OK, my darling, it'll be OK,

Jimmy – it feels like it won't be, but any minute now –

Amazing how you get through immediately. Rapid list of questions from the woman on the phone, but I can't understand them, I'm shaking and crying so hard.

Gary is being telephoned, the ambulance is coming.

I have this definite faith, this idea that they'll be able to revive Jimmy with their blue flashing lights and medication and coats, so why am I crying all over his small body, begging him to wait, but he's not listening?

How do I know this? Because bits of his laugh and smell and softly curving body are everywhere. His pale breath, his clean, curly frown and fat, kicky toes are flying up. Already his spirit's dancing off without me.

Eight

The airport was packed. You couldn't go to the toilet or get a coffee without queuing, and then it turned out the cappuccino machine was broken.

I decided to check in my bag – my arms were hurting and I was sweating too much to concentrate and also I was frankly scared of taking it on the plane. It was the nylon one – it may have been Gary's – with the strong zip and the fat sausage shape, and I'd fixed on a little padlock bought at the shop. It was hard, handing it over and as soon as I'd done it I knew it was a mistake.

Did you pack this bag yourself?

Yes.

Have you left it unattended for any period of time?

No.

Has anyone asked you to bring anything for them?

The woman bunged stickers on it and chucked it on the conveyor belt. My heart banged as I watched it disappear.

To calm myself, I went off and had a wander round the Duty Free. There were queues there, too. The chocolates were rubbish and over-priced, but I was tempted by the perfume in the shape of a pink cloud – more for the filmstar frosted bottle than the smell, which seemed to be of flower water gone bad. In the end I just got a massive pack of ciggies, enough to keep me going for a while.

The woman who served me had three long, dark

whiskers growing out of a mole on her cheek. I wondered why she didn't cut them. If they were mine I'd be itching to have a go with the nail scissors.

My breasts ached and prickled, so I went into the disabled toilet to relieve them. You got a basin to yourself in there, so I could squeeze and squirt and milk them to my heart's content.

They were so hot and hard it wasn't true, the sweat making the bra leave patterns on them. I was only feeding a couple of times a day, but it builds up if there's no one to suck. I held their heaviness, felt their rock hardness. Where is he? they were asking me, begging for his strong, busy lips and tongue.

The milk ran out, thin and blue, into the steel basin. Big relief. Someone's hairs were all over the basin – long grey ones. You wouldn't think someone could lose so much hair in just one visit to the toilet.

The lounge was a ripe spot for picking up punters – or would have been if I'd had the interest for it.

Men sat randomly alone with their elbows on their briefcases, staring, trousers scrunched up around their balls, patches of sweat under their arms. Wives and girlfriends elsewhere, minds on their dicks. Gins and tonics in a paper cup.

I fancied a stiff drink myself, but something stopped me. I'd got the Valium but I was scared to give up feeling things altogether, in case it led me somehow away from him.

I opened the ciggies and lit one, click. They all looked at you the moment you lit up – as if it meant something. The taste was chemical after the roll-ups I was used to. I inhaled and looked away at the strip of grey where the planes were lifting casually one by one into the sky.

Gary really went to pieces. What I'd liked about him was his emotional side, but all the same I didn't know a man could sob so hard. He held on to the furniture and moved himself around the flat like an old person, baffled and trying to stay upright.

I thought of how my husband could never have cried like that – how if this had happened to us, he'd have sat silently, in pieces but silent and shut. Then I remembered it had happened – to me – but the more Gary cried, the more I was tight and calm, a ball growing in my chest and an ache down my arm and into my shoulder, like something you couldn't prevent.

I kept remembering the day we'd registered Jimmy's birth. Gary with his big, chuffed arm around me, telling me jokes as I fed in the waiting-room, with all those new-born buggies everywhere. You knew they were new-born because their upholstery was so spanking new, their wheels so white and squeaky clean.

They gave me a sedative and a brown carton to be sick into and I lay down and as my edges grew fuzzy, we waited while they tried to find out what might have happened to make our little Jimmy die.

The room was white with a border of circus animals going round it and a box of beat-up toys in the corner. The window on the door was covered over and they were all very sensitive and considerate and acted like it was the most natural thing in the world to be howling one moment and lying face down and frozen up the next.

All the cups of tea were lined up going cold.

Gary tried to phone Harris again and again from the pay phone but there was no reply. I just couldn't tell him Harris had been round that day and helped look after Jimmy while I slept. The fact was a black lump on my heart that refused to translate into words. I decided Gary didn't have to know – how would it help anyone to know that?

I think he's gone away, I said after a while, without knowing why.

Gary stared at me with the tears all frozen in his eyes. Why? Why do you think that? What makes you say that, Amy?

I don't know, I said from somewhere inside my swollen up head, I just do.

On the plane, I took a couple of the Valium the doctor had given me. They worked surprisingly fast and I felt happily normal and blurred.

Headache? asked the blonde next to me. She kept on snapping her handbag open and shut and had been buzzing at me from the minute I sat down – one of those types that look around and try to catch your eye and you have to play the zombie to avoid them.

Not really, I said.

It's airless, she said. Recycled, unhealthy, isn't it?

She made a thing of looking out of the window at the tarmac, but really you could see she was dying to ask things. Her fingers gripped the seat where the radio buttons were. She had these long nails painted white to emphasise her tan, and no wedding ring, but then neither had I.

The noise of the engines got louder and the plane started to move. It was joltier than I'd expected and the noise was scary like something might explode. I felt some panic but I was hiding it well. The hostess was moving her hands around to indicate exits and holding a thing like a nosebag over her face. She indicated the straps and turned her head from side to side so you could see how she'd got it on.

To distract myself, I pulled out the laminated safety

card which was tucked in next to the sick bag. The diagrams were a laugh. I thought, who would get on to a plane with high heels anyway? And then I saw my friend had on little spiky ones, the sort which gave you a tipped-up dancer's foot. She'd certainly have to whip them off, I thought, if she was going to slide down the blow-up chute.

I'm going out to see my daughter, she said after a while.

Oh, I said.

She runs a taverna out there with her husband. Seven years she's been there. Two kids. Makes me feel like an old woman.

She chuckled. I nodded, but didn't reply.

You? she said.

Just a break, I told her.

On your ownsome?

I said nothing.

D'you mind if I have a look at your paper?

I gave it her. I hadn't looked at it and they were complimentary after all.

The plane took off and I heard the wheels bump up and tuck in. I couldn't help it, I gasped.

You don't like flying? she said.

It's OK.

I suppose I've just got used to it, she bragged. You OK?

I'm fine.

You're sure now?

I said yes and looked away out of the window where the earth had gone tipped and slanty. A few rows in front of us, a baby started up.

The morning after Jimmy died, I woke up with such a strong needing to hold him in my arms, dead or alive or whatever – that's all I knew, he had to be there,

175

ueezed next to my chest. I didn't care what state he
as in or whether it was a sensible plan.

I told Gary. I said it out loud to him even though he
was crying already – I don't think he'd been to bed. I
had. The sedatives had worked for me, though the
waking into the sharp scrape of the knowledge was
worse than no sleep. Gary was just sobbing and walking
around the flat, not knowing where to put himself.
Neither of us could settle our bodies into chairs, as a
normal person would.

I'm going there, I told him, I just am, that's where
I'm going, I don't care.

He looked at me.

He's ours, I reminded him carefully, I can't just leave
him there.

He opened his mouth to speak but what could he
say? He closed it again. If any words came out – and I
couldn't tell you now – it was to do with the pointless-
ness, the need to stay with him. But he didn't really
care, didn't really want me there in front of him,
reminding him.

I saw that in life we might now go our separate ways.

When we'd left the hospital the evening before,
walking politely away from his small body had seemed
the only thing to do. Our baby wasn't coming home
and that was that. There was nowhere solid for us to
be and soon the loss would make us strangers.

But now the idea of a white sheet over his little face,
it wasn't possible to bear it.

I want him, I told Gary, and it came out loud and
disturbing.

He held me, snatched at me, tried to keep me still.

No, I said, I'm serious. I really want him.

I was right. They were really very nice about it, very
understanding.

176

You're in shock, they said and someone straightaway put an arm around me. The arm had long, clean hairs all going the same way and it smelt of good habits and soap. I was going to fight it, but I didn't. It was good to be hugged by someone I'd never seen, the opposite of all I'd had to endure through my life.

Thanks, I said, the tears coming quickly.

The arm led me to a different room, a place with light pink flowers and a few magazines. I sat, looking at the wall and preventing my mind from going into areas which would shake me up. I hadn't eaten for so long I could taste my own juices, as if my body was dissolving from inside.

After a while they came to get me and I was taken to the room where he was, where he'd slept the night. It was a cold room. What a bad mother I felt.

Little Jimmy. I felt terrible that I'd waited till morning to come to my senses, that my stupidity had cost him a whole, lonely night. I thought of the minutes and the hours and the dark all around him. For a second, it bothered me that I hadn't thought to bring his changing bag or even a toy. Then I remembered. A twist gripped my innards like a period pain.

Has anyone been with him? I asked them. I hope he hasn't been left alone?

There's a high staff ratio here, they said.

I thought he'd be covered up, but to my relief his little face was showing and it was just the same but a lot less lively. He was still as an angel, my baby, with his blue eyelids and white forehead and that was suspicious, 'cause they never go that still and calm in real life. Straightaway my breasts started stinging, armpits hardening with stored up milk at the sight of his Jimmy face, his Jimmy look. I tried to control how starving I was for him. Milk was leaking, but it was OK, I'd been organised enough to put pads in.

All I want is to hold him for a bit, I said. Will that be possible?

I was taking such care to be polite and reasonable and not let my needs show up. It seemed important to let them know I knew who was boss. I was so worried they'd make trouble – try to prevent me from being with him or make me sign a form to part with him or something.

They said, did I want someone with me?

Oh, thanks, I said, That's really kind. But I think I'd rather be alone.

I discreetly wiped the tears off my chin.

Take your time, they said. And closed the door.

My bag was one of the first to come round and I pushed through the band of people all lighting up fags and got it off. It felt the same and the flimsy little padlock was still done up.

Have a nice holiday, said the woman from the flight, suddenly at my elbow. She'd lit up just like everyone else as soon as she was in the terminal and she had on a lightweight jacket which made her look different.

You take care now, she said like we were old buddies and I thanked her and was surprised that my arms were shaking so much. Maybe it was being so close to Jimmy.

It was hot outside – the thick blueness of the air hit you in the face and the lazy afternoon lull and petrol smell. Pink spiky flowers in dry soil in tubs and signs everywhere. Men in jackets with cigarette-smoking, robot faces were holding up cardboard with writing on.

In the dust I found a taxi and handed the man a piece of paper which had on it the name of the place where the ferry went from. I didn't even know 'yes' and 'no' in Greek.

English? he said. From London? You know Spice Girls?

I fall on him, breathe him in, but he doesn't smell right – he smells phoney, too clean, of someone else's soap. A cat or dog would lick it off and make it smell right again but I'm just a waitress and programmed in hygiene and good manners.

Otherwise, he's the same baby – same brownish crusts on his scalp, same fingernails that want cutting (he wouldn't let me near them with the scissors), same look on his face, except the eyes are so terribly closed. I don't dare open them, though it freaks me that I'll never see those bright baby eyes again.

He's wearing the sleepsuit Gary must have given them, white with the two balloons – a pink one and a green one, the strings overlapping – embroidered on the bib. It's not the one I'd have chosen and it's getting tight on the feet. I can tell by the soft bulk and the crackle that he has a nappy on, but there's a faint whiff and I wonder if it's clean.

He's not as stiff as I thought he'd be, but there's a bumpiness to holding him that doesn't feel good.

I clasp him so tight, kissing his small head, the bridge of his nose where the skin used to be warm and certain. I am crying, it's true, but without drama or terror or noise. All I want is more time, not much, just a reasonable amount – enough not to waste the feeling of loving my child. I'd like to push him back up inside me. My body would absorb him, hold him in, find his natural resting place.

I can't stand for him to go in the earth in a lonely grave.

A lot of Germans are on the ferry, drinking beer and laughing in their zip-up jackets. I hate their reddish

179

hair and their sun-pink skin and no eyelashes.

The afternoon's going, sliding to dusk. I stay on deck, to watch – keep my bag with me, in my arms, it's not that heavy. They all talk and shout and laugh and spit. I keep my distance, watch the horizon where the island's coming slowly into focus like an eye test: a sullen ridge of blue sticking out into the sea.

That's where I came from, I whisper to my bag.

The nurses who care for the dead wear clean, white clogs. They're so understanding, so respectful of my privacy, that they make the whole thing easy for me.

I've only got a PVC shopper with me, but he's a smallish baby, always was – he was low on that baby clinic chart from the word go. I wrap him carefully in the sheet just like when he was born. I don't like to cover his face. He won't quite lie flat on the bottom of the shopper, so I sort of sit him. I hold the bag clasped to my chest – you see them held that way all the time when people are in a rush or carrying groceries or something.

It's not wrong, just unexpected. How was I to expect it? Dealing with the unexpected is half of life – the unkind half no one else can help you with.

I am sweating and I feel sick and am in a spin about meeting someone in the corridor. A nurse passes me, but she's looking at her watch and I glance at the doors as though I know my way.

I do know my way. A new knowingness has settled on me. A taxi takes us home – the tip I give him is so big it's almost not funny.

And my feet touched this land, not for the first time.

Palm trees swaying, white walls, blue shutters and a castle up above like a fort. Aphrodite's island, Harris had said, She came here because it was on the way to nowhere.

Aphrodite?

No, Jody. Aphrodite was born out of the foam – you know, like in the famous picture? She just sped along on her shell and then walked out of the sea. A beautiful image, don't you think?

I didn't care about images.

Like my mother walked into it? I said, and he gave me a look.

Dust blew off the quay – the Germans huddled there with their rucksacks and maps. Having a discussion about what to do next.

I knew what I was doing next. I couldn't remember the last time I'd eaten anything, so I went straight over to the blue-painted chairs and gingham tables and sat down.

I was too hot in my leggings and shirt but the hotness was pleasant and luxurious almost, warming up my bones. I felt suddenly OK and on top of things – nothing would be that hard any more. In a different land it was harder to miss Jimmy, but anyway my grief had turned off a part of me and I preferred it that way.

I looked around me, felt the sun on my arms, the unusual feeling of sunglasses pressing on my nose, the breeze. There was a sound of insects in the bushes and some kids were kicking a ball around. The youngest was a boy, black sticky-up hair and big front teeth. I felt tears coming to my eyes but I stopped them, concentrated on the café.

The PVC cloths were clipped to the tables and a sign in English said, 'Don't touch the lamps'. It was funny how everything was in English. You had to keep on batting the wasps away.

In the square beyond, a little bell was dinging. It all looked much like a postcard, with the blueness and

181

the shadows. There were signs for Coca-Cola and Seven-Up.

I put the bag carefully under the table between my feet and looked at the menu. A photo of pizza and another one of fish and chips. I thought that perhaps I should have walked further away from the ferry, but it was too late now, the man had seen me and anyway my stomach was caving in with hunger.

When he came over, I smiled and said, Greek food, please, and he winked and got the pad from his pocket.

I watched the ferry leave with a low toot and a puff of smoke and as it got quickly further away, the man brought over a big, chipped plate of tomato and cucumber chopped up in oil and some hard bread and yellowish wine. The tomato was the best I've ever tasted, the flavour clinging to your mouth as you swallowed.

I ate slowly. The wine tasted of nail cleaner but you got used to it and it made my head empty and warm in the sun. As I ate, I made sure not to think about anything – not Gary or Harris or the aloneness or what I had to do. I had some drachmas but I was going to have to cash a traveller's cheque.

From London? said the man as I paid him, and I said no and asked him where Diakofti was.

He pointed vaguely at the church. Other side, he said, Long way. You want shower?

No, thanks, I said. Taxi.

He shrugged. Mike's Bikes, he said.

Mike's Bikes?

He pointed to a building which said OTE in big letters. Then he counted up the money and went away.

It was urgent to get to Diakofti. I was worrying about Jimmy going bad in the heat.

I walked over to where the OTE sign was.

Mike's Bikes was a man in roughly his thirties who spoke quite good English.

He didn't seem surprised to see me. He cashed my cheque for me and I put the drachmas carefully away in my bag, thinking I'd spend some time later getting used to the currency. I'd never had foreign money in my hand before. It was surprising how unreal it felt.

Do you mind if I say you are a sexy lady? he said, and I could tell he was looking at my hair – straggled and unwashed as it was – because you didn't see too many blondes out here.

I looked at his Levi's and vest and tanned dusky skin and black hairs sprouting out all over even at his throat and from his ears, and I showed him on the map where I wanted to go.

Diakofti? he said, opening out his hands in surprise.

Yes. Diakofti. How can I get there?

He frowned and flicked the map in a pissed off way with a finger.

Not go to Diakofti, he said. Why? There is nothing. You stay here and we go in nightclub-bar-disco and have a good time, booze a lot and eat pizza.

Thanks, I said, But I need to get to Diakofti. Today.

You stay there? he asked me doubtfully.

I nodded.

He sighed, shrugged. OK, sexy lady, he said, I drive you. In superb truck.

There was a truck. The back of it was covered in crates of fruit and two chickens were pecking about in the dirt by the wheels. He kicked the chickens and they scattered then straightaway came back for more.

I drive you, he said. Is OK. Anywhere you want to go.

I hadn't time to worry.

He indicated that he had to get the fruit and veg into the shade. He brought me a glass of something and I drank it. It was like the nail cleaner, only more reddish.

I tried to pay, but he held my arm.

We are good friends, he said. We go dancing and for hamburger.

You visit for a holiday? he said when I climbed up beside him.

I was born here, I said. It was the first time I'd said those words aloud on the island and it felt like the truest and most spectacular thing I'd told anyone for a long time.

He took his hands off the wheel in amazement and the truck swerved for a second across the dirt track.

You have Greek family? he said. Brothers? Father?

No, I shook my head, English mother, but she died.

The bag is starting to smell – not surprising with the heat and so on. After I left the hospital and got home, I only gave myself half an hour to get some things and pick up that passport Harris had blessedly got me. I was panting with the effort of hurrying. I couldn't risk Gary getting back from wherever he was.

I unwrapped Jimmy and sure enough, his nappy – a plain white hospital one, much too small – was a bit dirty. Someone had put it on too tight – maybe in a hurry when they knew I was coming, there were red marks on his light baby skin.

I spoke soothingly to him as I wiped him down and put on a fresh Pampers, thinking this is the last time I'll do this for him – press down the tape, get it nice and straight and not too tight. He seemed to be smiling, but I badly didn't want his sweet mouth to open. He was still my baby, but he was something else as well and I didn't know what that was or whether I liked it.

I re-wrapped him and packed him among my things, at the centre of the hold-all, where my clothes would protect him from bumps. There was some rosebud pot-pourri in a dish above the toilet and it suddenly occurred to me to toss that in the bag. It was a bit dusty, but it had a sweet antiquey smell and might help make everything a bit nicer.

I was doing the sensible thing and taking the Valium the doctor had given me. I hadn't missed a pill. It was amazing for making your limbs feel smooth, your head comfy and slow. I'd never had anything like it before. Without it, I don't know how I'd have coped.

The island of my birth made the UK seem so dark and miserable and tight. I thought of how often I'd taken those thick horizons and hard, crowded roads for granted. Now I was open to the heaven I'd come from – sprung, if you want, like Aphrodite in the picture: everything lovely and beautiful like the best stories.

The colours were bright and firm like out of a good dream and the skies were stuffed with colour and the heat stroked your face and softened your heart. I could see why Jody had gone there. The heavy scent and smudge of the flowers got in my mouth and I felt alive and uncaring and almost happy. I knew it was the right thing, too, bringing Jimmy to this place.

What would they have done when they found him gone from the hospital? I imagined Gary rushing there, imagined all the different possibilities of his reaction and felt truly sorry when I thought of the pain this would give him – pain he didn't deserve, no way.

I thought about Gary a lot. I still loved him, but the place where I kept that love was out of reach to me now. I did not want to reach it. The idea of doing that would have wiped me out. In taking Jimmy, I'd got the little bit of Gary I wanted.

If anyone knew anything about the world, there'd be no worrying. Even Gary ought to know. He's with his mum, he'd say, No harm can come to him now.

After a few miles, Mike's Bikes put his hand on my thigh.

You like ouzo? he said, grinning away like the dumb idiot he was.

I wouldn't know, I said, Haven't had it.

He smacked his lips: Is best Greek drink, best in the world.

I shuffled my legs so his hand was off me. I didn't want to risk offending him, but we were climbing steeply now and I wanted him to concentrate on the road. Me and Jimmy ending up at the foot of a cliff was not part of my plan. There were a surprising amount of pylons, the wires hanging down wildly in places – I couldn't work them out. It did not seem like a place with so much electricity.

The sand on the road was almost red and the dust flew up all the time. To our right, there was a sheer drop down to the sea. I couldn't look at it without feeling giddy, yet it was such a view. I wished I had a camera. The sun was sliding into the sea which was perfectly striped: turquoise, navy and black.

So you are good Greek girl? Mike's Bikes said again.

Well, not really, I said, but I couldn't be bothered to explain it all.

Greek wife and mother is the best, he said, nodding to himself. In Greece you know where you come from. In England, you die and you are forgotten.

I smiled, but inside you could say I was angry. I wanted to tell him, no one was going to forget my baby.

I like Greece, I said, It's a good place – and then I wished I hadn't said it because he put his hand back on my knee.

The bag was very sniffy, but Mike's Bikes didn't seem to have noticed. His mind was firmly on his cock as all men's are. I relaxed and ignored him. I needed all my strength for finding a place to sleep and to bury my child.

Is Diakofti, he said all of a sudden, though nothing to my mind seemed to have changed.

I leaned forward and looked. We were going down even more steeply, the tyres shaking over even rougher ground than before. Little stones slipping. On a bend, someone had left a bunch of flowers in a jar by the roadside. A bird called from somewhere, a fed-up, put-out little cry.

I sighed without knowing why.

Many bad things in this place, said Mike's Bikes dramatically, his hand spidering back up my leg.

What bad things? I said.

He shrugged, moved his thumb back and forward on my thigh. Bad killings, he said, And so on –

Tell me, I said, letting his hand stay there.

He made a big, put-on face as if the words hurt as they came out, and said, Baby died, got its head smash in, you know?

What baby? I said.

Electricity snagged up my spine and he bunched his lips: Some little child. Better to forget it, you know?

I said nothing. I was sick of him saying 'you know?' when I didn't really know anything – in fact he was getting on my wick in every way. I stared at the land, thick with shadows, falling away beneath us.

You like babies? said Mike's Bikes after a minute and licked his lips.

Not specifically, I said and I knew he wouldn't understand the word and I didn't care a fuck.

Soon, I thought, soon I'll see something I recognise.

But there were just more pylons and bushes with the hissing getting louder.

Then we came round a sharp corner and you saw the smooth cup shape of the bay, the end of the sun. Rays of pink above the flatness of the water, a couple of boats far out. And in front, a strip of silvery sand like out of a holiday brochure, which bit sudden and hard into my heart.

I've been here! I told Mike's Bikes – I couldn't help myself, it just came out – I know this beach!

But he wasn't listening at all – he'd slipped his hand right in between my thighs and was moving upwards looking for the zip.

In the Garden for the Blind, I used to cut myself into pieces – one for you, one for you – and it was easy enough once I'd got the courage up to start. Who was to say if my body was or wasn't mine? In the end, it all comes back to you: limbs, hair, a smile and a spurt of semen. A chance to put off death.

I drew out all my money in one go in the end, thick in my hand. I thought it would feel powerfully exciting, marvellous, but in fact it was only so-so.

Mike's Bikes seemed to think I was going to be his girlfriend. I take you for ouzo, he said enthusiastically. Tomorrow?

I shook my head.

After tomorrow? he said.

Not tomorrow, I replied, Not after tomorrow. Not ever.

Some other time, then?

Never, I said. Sorry, mate.

I could have let Mike's Bikes fuck me, of course I could, or could have bent down and blown him. That's what he thought was going to happen – Yes, baby, he kept on saying, rubbing at my leggings, Go on, baby, yes, yes.

I've only ever had sex with one man and not felt used.

He was fairly snarling with it by the time we pulled in to a little, black grove of trees where the shade buzzed and hummed around us. He shoved his hands up inside my shirt, felt my tits resting in my bra, hard and cramped up with milk. I wasn't going to explain that to him.

A sharp lump of granite stuck up out of the ground in front of us.

Memorial for atrocities of the war, he explained – half tour guide, half sex-maniac – as he yanked my knickers down. I kept my hands on the bag the whole time and regretted that perhaps the Valium had made me too easy-going. In the end I began to laugh.

Wait, I said, I need to go.

He frowned and gripped my wrists.

Pee pee, I said, indicating my crotch. Bladder full.

I got out of the truck, taking Jimmy with me, and I saw Mike's Bikes settle back and start to take his trousers down.

Next to the big lump of war granite were a whole lot of little lumps about the size of cannon balls arranged in a circle. I picked up a heavy one and walked back to the truck.

He was fine when I left him – bleeding heavily and a bit confused and swearing and shouting at me in his mother tongue. All that smart English had gone by the board and his trousers and pants were off and the brown worm of his cock hung down stupidly between his legs.

I made sure I didn't do enough damage to send him running to the police, but a few brain cells less wasn't going to make a big difference.

His blood had specked my shirt, but there were bigger things to worry about. The light was fading and it would soon be evening. My sandals kicked up dust as I walked down to Diakofti. I wondered how long his truck would stay parked there. He had nothing on me, but all the same I wondered how long I'd got.

There were olive trees on either side of the path and then some stumps with paper bags over them. I wondered why. Someone had put a chair – painted blue like in a child's painting – upside down in a tree. Why did it look familiar and make my stomach slide to one side? Then the path curled round and I saw the fisherman's shack.

And that, too, stirred something in me – like a dog's tail, thumping, then still, then thumping again.

It was a low white building with a slanting awning made of bamboo and other twigs. A few tables and chairs. Red and blue plastic beer crates piled up. A beat-up motorbike leaning against the wall – a black tyre, a blue Calor gas thing.

The ground was wet as if freshly hosed. There was no sound, no sign of anyone. But I knew without having to ask that this was my old home.

I stood for several minutes and then an old man came out, one finger stuck up his nose. He paused at seeing me, left the finger there, then pulled it out and wiped it on his trousers. He must have just been asleep because his braces hung down around his knees. He had on black knee-boots and a brown drooping cardigan, even in this heat.

He looked at me and his face didn't give any signs.

A room to rent? I said.

He said nothing.

You have a room? I said slowly. I put the bag down

at my feet. My shoulders were killing me.

He nodded as if he understood, but carried on standing there.

A place to stay? I said.

He relaxed and laughed suddenly – black hole instead of teeth.

Then Gary stepped out of the shadows behind him.

Nine

Gary spoke fast to the man. He spoke in Greek.

I sank down on to an empty beer crate and pulled the bag in closer to my legs and all the things I'd never understood clustered together so fast I felt sick. I put my fingers on my forehead and tears seemed to whoosh down just like that, unasked for and without anywhere to go.

Now and then Gary looked over at me, but it was like someone else looking.

The old man went over and coiled up the hose, then said something to Gary and walked away. Gary came to me.

He seemed to have a different walk now, more thoughtless and relaxed – or else it was just the same and I'd never examined it in the right way before. I stared at him and then I took my eyes away, I couldn't bear it. Oh yes, I thought as I saw that his clothes were different and he had on the bashed-up leather sandals with a loop for the toe to go through, that I'd seen the men at the port wearing.

He was full of shock, too, choked up with it, I could tell that – but he knew what he was doing.

Amy, he went – and then when I couldn't speak, he bent and touched my hair and said, I'm so sorry to do this. It's not what you think, none of it is.

I pushed his hand from my head because its caring touch hurt me. What do I think? I said.

I don't know – and I could see all the grief of our

baby still contained there in his different, foreigner's eyes – I don't know what you think, he said.

I tried to say more but couldn't – my voice was so washed away by recent events – gone from where it normally came out.

Come here, he said, though we were already so close up to each other it stung.

I did nothing, but he crouched down and surrounded me with the normal bigness of his arms. It's OK, he said, It's OK, it's me, I'm here. Don't cry.

I wasn't crying. The beer crate jittered a bit as he pulled me carefully into him. I could hear the sound of chewing and I smelled something sharp on him, foreign things I didn't recognise.

I pushed him off me after a minute or two.

I flew, he said.

I saw his big body streaming through the air and gazed without understanding at the shape of the words. I remembered Jimmy's small, curled sleep on the sheet at the hospital, how I'd wrapped him so neatly and escaped down the corridor – how it had been him and me from then on and how bad and wrongly done it had felt, giving him up to the hold on the plane.

That's how I got here before you, he said. I got a small plane from Athens. There's an airport at Viaradika, well – 'airport' – it's actually more of a landing strip –

He said the words in the Greek way, chewing them up till they were changed and foreign. I saw that it was all natural to him – gum shifting in his mouth, rocking back on his dusty heels.

He was probably looking at me and he tried to take my hands, but I wouldn't let him, he wasn't getting off that easily, when I couldn't move or speak.

He blotted a tear of mine with a finger and said, You knew there was something, didn't you?

194

He stood with his hands in his shorts pockets, look
at the dark sea. I still sat on the crate. Everything was
coming at me and I couldn't get a hold on it.

I understand that you can't speak to me right now,
he was saying, That you can't stand to look at me, but
all this time I've been on your side. I tried to tell you
so many times. I always failed, always. I loved you. I'm
sorry.

I thought about this and couldn't begin to calculate
what it meant. And then I saw there was no point in
bothering. I had always known only what he and Harris
meant me to know. Terrible amounts of grief were
rolling over me. I was out of breath with the weight of
what was going on.

After a while, a woman appeared with her sleeves
rolled up, and some brown children jumping up and
down. The woman was fatter than Gary and her skirt
had been done up with a safety pin and she carried a
big, hefty, brown-haired baby. But as soon as she put
him on the ground, he turned into a toddler who ran
and yelled and chased the scabby chickens. Everyone
seemed to know Gary. He pulled the children's hair
and laughed and played with them. I looked away. I
couldn't watch his hands on another child. The sounds
flew back and forward and I began to understand that
he was Greek.

I still couldn't speak to him. I didn't want to discuss
what was in my bag.

We all sat down. He messed around with the kids
but he kept his eyes on me. Then he rolled a cigarette
– I watched him do it without thinking, just as if he
did it every day – and held it out to me. I took it and
fished out my own lighter. Then he did one for himself.
He's never smoked, went a voice in my head. Never
and now he does.

I've lost everything, I thought.

After a while, the old man came back and said something.

He wants you to go with him, Gary said in a careful voice which was supposed to make me trust him. He'll show you your room.

I picked up the bag and as I moved it some pong spilled out. Jesus, fuck, the pot-pourri wasn't doing any good any longer. Maybe it was the nylon making the contents sweat. We walked up some little steps and round the back of the shack away from the water, towards the mountain. I couldn't help wondering if it was going to be my mum's room. To our left was the vegetable patch I'd been born in – don't ask me how I knew it, I just did. Parts of me were buried in there, and the rambling, dirt square of earth called out to me as I passed.

The man jabbered away as he walked, but it was more to himself than to me. I wanted to look back and see if Gary was still sitting there smoking, but I didn't.

The room was smallish and bare and quite dirty – the bed had one worn-out blanket and there were dark stains on it. A wooden crucifix hung over the bed and gave me the shivers. Yellowed splotches of insects flecked the grubby walls, an unlit spiral mosquito repeller on the sill.

The old man said a few things and I nodded and smiled. There didn't seem to be any questions in what he said so I felt no need to answer any. He pointed to my hair and I held the end of my plait out and made the sound of laughing. It was a long time since my voice had done that and it sounded put-on and weird in the little, dirty room. The man tried to take my bag from me, but I hung on and said, Ochi, ochi – learned, funnily enough, from Mike's Bikes – my one word of Greek.

Then I tried to ask for the toilet and he grinned. I did an act of squatting to pee and he roared with laughter and pointed around the side of the building. I was glad we'd hit it off. He might have known my mother, after all. And Paul, and me.

I put the bag on the bed and went round and pissed half standing up as the toilet was filthy with shit and I don't know what else. It stank and there was no light and no paper to wipe yourself.

The sea was practically licking at the toilet door. It had grown darker and was calm and the sand went on forever like a brochure. Behind me, small mountains came up out of the darkness. The air up there would be cool and clean.

I thought of ghosts, Gary, his sudden Greekness, and felt the true thud of my loss. The inside of my mouth was eaten up with the shock.

When I got back to the room, one of the kids was kneeling on the bed, having a go at unzipping my bag. Jesus! I couldn't believe it. I had the key, but all the same.

I screamed at him to get the fuck out and he began to cry loudly, his face broken up. He didn't know Jimmy was in there. He cried and then I found myself crying too and I sat down and saw how dirty my hands were, like old gypsy woman hands and how it was in another life that I'd last bothered to take a look at them.

Gary came and stood in the doorway, his skin looking browner already and his eyes red like he'd cried and expected to cry more.

I bashed a man, I told him loudly, With a rock. I may have hurt him.

He smiled sadly as if it was funny. Mike's Bikes? he said and did a sweeping away gesture with his hand.

Don't worry. We pay him to get you here and he still fucks it and you end up walking the last bit.

I wanted to – I began to say, and then broke off as I understood what he was telling me. I moved away from him.

I never did anything to you, he said softly, grasping his two hands as if they were going to rebel against his big, careful body.

Is Harris here, too? I asked him and he looked upset and touched the door gently with the tip of his thumb.

Why d'you ask that? he said.

Just answer me.

My voice was hard, I knew it was. It was Jimmy and me now. The rest could dissolve into space.

I'm not scared of you, Gary, I said. Just tell me where Harris is.

Gary said, He may be here, Amy. The truth is I don't know – that is the real truth of the situation, I swear. We must think quickly –

Why must we? About what?

About what we do if he is.

I'm not doing anything with you, I told him, even though I knew already he would ignore me. I've done enough with you. I'm sick of doing, doing with fuck-all information to go on –

I was crying and then I wasn't.

I know, he said. Don't tell me what I already know.

He made no move towards me this time, but he put his head deep in his hands, squatted in that doorframe.

Where's Jimmy? he whispered and there was a split in his voice, sharp as a cut.

Nowhere, I told him but as I said it I couldn't stop myself flicking a look at the bag where it sat on the bed.

He came closer to me and I could smell him. For the first time I noticed that his arms weren't only fat, they were strong as well, the muscles curved like animals sleeping under the skin. He went to the bed and laid his hands on the bag and I saw him wipe his wrist across his eyes.

Good for you, he said to me, Bringing him.

Go fuck yourself, I told him – wanting to punish him for showing me that everything in my life had been far from my control, fully formed before it happened, hidden behind great rolling lumps of time.

Amy – he put his hands in my raggy, greasy hair, Amy –

I put my mouth on his shoulder and I bit, not hard but not soft either. He let me, he didn't flinch or move away.

I'm sick of you knowing everything, I said. I pulled back his shirt and I bit again and this time I felt the flesh snap, and he gasped and I tasted blood.

Of course you are, he said and now he was crying.

Already a mosquito was whining. Things flowed between us again.

Gary said it was important to act normally so he made me eat supper under the awning with the little kids and the old man and the fat woman who was probably young, but had a body that was sliding off out of her reach into old age.

I asked him at one point if she was his sister or even his wife, but he frowned and said, I don't come from here. My sister's in Athens.

The one with the baby? I said as surprise went over his face.

Not such a baby now.

I was getting used to the wine and the old man kept fussing at me and filling up my glass, but I couldn't eat. The children were throwing fir cones under the

199

crates and then fishing them out again. It seemed to be a game they did a lot.

The smallest, a girl with her hair in bunches, came up to me and put a cone in my hand. I closed my fingers around it and she got cross when I wouldn't let it go. She stamped her foot and everyone laughed as I passed it back to her. I didn't get it into her hand until the fifth time of trying. Maybe it didn't show, but I was finding I could no longer let go of things.

They know who you are, Gary said, putting his arm around me, squeezing me to him, Panos remembers you. The blonde angel, he calls you.

Once or twice during the evening I went back to my room to check on the bag. It was just as I had left it, on the bed, surrounded by nothing. A quick cuddle was tempting but I just had to make do with hugging the bag.

The smell didn't bother me any more, just as your own smells don't bother you, you're immune to your own piss and shit, the slow brown fustiness of your own blood.

I had terrible hankerings. I so wanted to get Jimmy's face out to look at one last time, but I was frightened of it not keeping so well in the heat and I didn't want to see him looking different or ugly or bad.

What are you hoping to do? Gary asked me in my room.
Do?
With him.
My fingers and heart were shaking so much I couldn't answer. I let out a quick sob and put my hand up to feel for tears. Wetness was there all right. I had lost track of when I was crying or not all the time.
Say the name, I told him, Say what you're saying. Do with who?

I knew it hurt him too much to say it. I knew it, but I wanted to feel him hurt. I'd carried that bag. I'd carried that baby.

Tell me what, Gary was begging now, I know you're wanting to do something. Tell me what it is you want and I'll help you, before Harris finds us.

He's here, then?

I told you, I don't know. I don't want him near – Jimmy –

Gary broke off, shaky. He put his fist in his mouth, looked around the room all the time, like he was trying to work out what to do with me and our baby.

Are you going to bury him? – he spoke to me very gently as if I was an innocent person with good ideas – Is that what you came to do? Answer me, Amy. I have to know.

Why do you have to know?

He's mine too.

Something inside me was sinking. He's no one's, I said. He's not any one's any more. Are you, Jimmy? I said to the bag.

Gary sat on a chair by the wall and scratched away at something with his fingers. Maybe it was wax that had dripped from a candle. Maybe he wanted to pull the wall down, crumb by crumb.

I have to tell you something, he said at last.

I don't want to know, I said quickly, but he told me all the same.

Thinking back over the last year, what comes to me first?

I'd like to say it was the proud, tight bloom of my love for Gary and the birth of our beautiful child, but no, it is walking through those pale streets, work and garlic and fat clinging to my shirt and my hair – walking to meet Harris in some pub or room or tea shop, where

201

he will lean back and laugh and speak the secrets I want to hear.

He never took from me. He handed my life back to me. He made sense of what I never knew I had. He made up such brilliant stories.

Your mother killed her own child, Amy.

Paul? I said. It's not true.

Gary clasped his hands together and stared down at the floor.

Look at me, I said – and he looked up slowly and I saw that it was true.

She threw him against a wall. She fractured his skull.

This wall?

No. Not this wall.

Why?

Gary sighed a long sigh. It's not for me to say. But she was sick, wasn't she, your mum? You know that, Amy. You've always known that. She killed herself afterwards.

I stared at him. I don't want to know, I heard myself say.

What you want to know and what you know, they're two different things.

Shut up, I told him, and then ideas speeded up in my mind. Harris knows all about this?

Gary kept his eyes on mine. He was Paul's father, Amy.

But –

He gave me a long look, but he didn't try to come near me. I think you knew these things, he said.

I said nothing. I couldn't see inside my own head any more. All I could see was his big, anxious face looking at me. And my mother. And the ways I was like her.

She killed their child, he said. And then she walked into the sea.

Here at Diakofti? I said even though I knew it.

Here. Just down the beach, beyond – you know, beyond the pines.

I said nothing.

He totally fucking adored Jody, but she wouldn't have him, didn't really want his child. She knocked herself about a bit, to try to lose it, but it clung on and got itself born –

I helped her with Paul, I said suddenly and it was like I was hearing my own small voice, my big girl helping on the beach voice.

Gary smiled, then his face went serious again. When he came looking for you in the city, he told you a lot of lies, Amy. He didn't care for you or what you thought, except to keep you coming round to the house. He would do anything to attract you, brutal things. Even though sometimes he could hardly bear to look at you. I thought you must see that – that you reminded him of her?

Sometimes you know things, I said, but they don't matter in that way.

I sat next to Jimmy on the bed, my body trembling, my teeth knocking in my head as if they wouldn't stop.

Why – what did he – want to do? I said.

Gary didn't answer me.

What? I said again, louder.

After – Jimmy – came, Gary went on, I used to worry. It wasn't in the plan. He threw us together for fun, you see, to keep you around the house. Sex was OK – he thought, well, he found that a bit of a laugh – but he never meant us to love each other and he certainly never meant us to have a child, and then –

I looked at him and saw how bad and hard and hopeless love was.

A baby boy, Gary went and stopped, prevented from speaking for how hard he was crying.

203

I'm sorry, I whispered, understanding he was griev-
ing, but unable to go and touch him.

When I remember Jimmy's last hours, it's another time,
separate and cut away from this one. First, I was a
skulking girl – living my mean life with my husband,
chopping and snipping at work, doing the blow-jobs
for the men in the park, walking the streets of the
greyish city, secret and contaminated.

Then Harris found me – who cares why or how? –
and then Gary. After we'd made love, his juices would
fall from me and I couldn't get them back in fast
enough. Then I was a mother and love was handed
over to me on a plate. Love and happiness.

Gary could see what I was thinking. He sees my
thoughts before I do. He sees me sitting there, hands
folded in my lap, and he says, Look at you, Amy.

I know, I say.

You've changed.

I know.

Changed and grown, I thought, But all it does is
open you up for more grief.

Gary knows. He knows what my plans are. I nod at
him before he can say anything.

Don't bury him out there, he says, and I know he
means the vegetable patch with its black, dug-up earth
and memories of my first breaths.

I flush.

You wouldn't get the hole deep enough – it's a big
deal, digging a grave, Amy, you've no idea – he'd, he'd
– well, he'd be discovered the first time Panos turned
the potatoes over.

I don't want to bury him, I say, I want to –

What?

He waits. I begin to cry again and this time Gary comes
over and takes me in his arms and holds me tight as a

204

love story and I try to get out short bursts of words, explaining what I want to do with his and my child.

I want to put him somewhere where his face –

Gary holds my shoulders and looks into mine.

His face?

Where his face doesn't have to be covered up.

Gary says he knows a place.

He shifts the bag to the floor which has a thin brown mat curling at the edges. He says he should stay in my room with me tonight.

I don't want you, I tell him, but he says he won't leave me and when he takes off his Greek clothes and his fat, bare body creaks into the bed next to me, it is almost like home and all the bad things haven't come between us.

Shutting my eyes, I can imagine up our baby boy still there for us in the cherrywood crib, arms flung above his head, breathing easily.

Harris came over, I tell him, That afternoon – the afternoon Jimmy –

I know, Gary whispers, I know –

His hands are on my face, but I pull away. How do you know? I ask him, How can you –?

I know you, he says, I know when you're leaving things out. I can hear the truth between the words you say to me.

I didn't say anything to you –

I know you didn't.

Jimmy's death is getting closer now, a dark shape moving over us, next to us, into us. I want it. I will have any part of Jimmy that's on offer.

He failed to breathe, Gary says, making my heart jump – Sudden infant death –

They don't know, I tell him quickly. They never did any tests or cut him open.

Well, he says, You took him away, didn't you – didn't you, Amy?

He didn't die of not breathing, I tell Gary, remembering his sweat and my shouting and the sleep he slid into just to please me.

Gary touches my body, holds parts of me, then moves on to other parts. He puts his hand on my bottom, slides it down to where my thighs should be – only all those things turned away from me a long time ago. My cunt is a long ago thing. I will never get my body back, I know that now.

Harris, I tell him, tell myself, Was trying to help.

Harris, he says, Has never in his life tried to help.

What?

You heard what I said.

My face has got used to the tears running over it now. Gary leans on his elbow to light the mosquito spiral and blows out the candle. I move towards him in the new dark, touched by habit, untouched by desire.

Ahhh, he goes, rubbing my shoulders and – That's it. That's better. My girl, my Amy, my love.

He notices I'm wearing a bra in bed and he touches my breasts gently. The touch makes the milk spring out, a fizzy prickle, a greedy ache, getting less now.

Poor girl, he goes, and he slides a hand between my legs, not in a sexual way but just as I would myself, for comfort.

The silence ticks in our ears.

Jimmy's with us now, Gary says and I don't know how to answer him. There's no answer to give. I don't know what to think – about Harris, about anything.

Jimmy's death rushes past us, terrible, but trying to go.

What did he want? I ask the fat man as we lie pressed together in darkness.

What did Harris want? he repeats as the moments
fill up the air. He takes a breath, thinking about it. To
get one back on Jody, he says at last – and scared
thoughts creep up my spine. Revenge. Sport. To make
me do things –

Things?

To you. Things to you. You must realise, Amy, he's a
spectator.

I liked him, I say simply.

Yes, you did.

So – what? – you're saying he might be here now?

Gary says nothing, draws me closer.

Answer me.

I don't know, he says at last, I don't understand him,
Amy. I haven't known him long.

Jesus – I feel my whole body clench – Jesus, Gary –

He shifts in the bed, moves his arms up so they
meet around me. I smell his neck and chest and the
familiar bitter hotness under his arms.

No time at all, he whispers, ashamed and relieved. I
met him here on the island, a year ago.

But – I pull my face away, trying to fix on his eyes in
the darkness.

I'm Greek, Amy, he says, I'm not English. I hid it
well, didn't I?

All my thoughts were still filled up with Jimmy. How
was I to care what Gary was? I remembered all the
times I'd found him strange, the picked-out way of
speaking, the times he didn't seem to know what was
what – the child he became in shops, streets. I knew
nothing of the world. How could I compare the things
that were different about him to the things I didn't
know?

I lied to you, Gary said. No, not lied. Left it out. You
never asked. I make a good Englishman.

But –

My mother was English – from Birmingham. She fell for my father on holiday, usual story. I grew up in Athens.

I say nothing, watch the pictures changing and laughing at me in my head.

OK, he says, Thirteen to eighteen, it's true, I was in the UK. A shitty public school – her family money.

And then I hear it. He says a word like shitty but he shows it off like a foreigner, makes me uneasy, like I can't believe him. Yet I never saw it before.

He waits for a beat.

It's not that hard, he says slowly, Telling you all this. And yet it's all over. Knowing this, you can leave me.

I was quiet.

Can't you, Amy? It makes you able to leave me?

I want to hear the story, I said. It was the second time I'd heard a story. I remembered the slip-slidey feel of being in Harris's room more than a year ago, of hearing his voice describing pictures in my head, his hands moving to make things seem true or reasonable, my head resting on the furniture of his room.

I came back, said Gary. I started a law course in Athens, worked a bit for my father – he was building a house on the island – this island – for the family, only I wouldn't live in it. Pig-headed, you know? I was planning to go to America – get into one of those big firms with views and mile-high glass windows. Back home, my father ran a fucking bar and my mother helped him. Her family had hated that she married him and her mother-in-law hated her. Now she was making the best of it. She said other people were worse off. I can imagine a different life, she said, but what's the point in doing that?

Like my mother, I said.

No, he said. Your mother changed things. Mine stayed put. And the house stayed unfinished and my

208

mother had just the sheep for company. In the summer months they didn't see each other, and in the winter months he drank and laid bricks. They didn't even have a fucking living-room. She slept with chickens coming and going, a dirt floor –

As Gary told me these things, I realised no one had told me much truth in my life. What had I done to deserve so many lies, so many believable stories?

And? I said.

And then I did something I shouldn't have.

He stopped speaking and I heard his breath in the darkness.

Everyone does things, I told him.

No, said Gary. This was really something.

And?

And Harris was – Harris knew my father, Harris knew what I did. He didn't tell anyone, he was un-believably generous with cash. He took me back with him –

Why? I say quickly.

Why? Gary breathes. Aren't you going to ask what I did?

I don't care what you did. Why did he do all that?

I can't answer that, I don't know. He took me to London.

He shivers and I can feel he's crying.

It's OK, I tell him, Don't –

All this time – you don't see it, Amy – Harris said I'd lose you if you found out.

What was it, then, some kind of crime?

He pauses, kisses my cheek. It was a crime, yes, it was. It was a crime.

I don't care what you did, I say again because I don't want to hear and I'm afraid and I can tell that we're both getting our breath, so scared of each other in this bed and all the wild facts circling us.

I was lonely, he says, I never had much luck with girls. He laughs, he kisses me again. I was – look at me – a fat man.

You're a wonderful size, I say quickly, as he knows I will.

He cries a little. And I keep on listening as he says, I met this – person –

I begin to laugh.

No, he says, You don't get it. I met a boy. I was in a bar for blokes, for – boys.

You like – boys?

He hesitates. I liked – anyone who –

You wanted –?

Yes Amy, I wanted a fuck, is that so bad?

I laugh a little bit more and then, out of respect for him, I stop.

Silence. The sea beating close by in our ears. Our baby, the bag, the bed.

I knew you'd be like that, he said.

Like what?

Unconcerned, think it was OK, what I did –

If you knew –

Why didn't I tell you? Why didn't I tell you? Why? Why? he said to himself, and while he was thinking about it, I pushed my head into his chest, smelt the closeness of his few, unshowy hairs.

We've all done things, I said.

I thought I – I didn't know. I was in a bad way generally.

So – what? You fucked him?

Amy, Jesus, I fucked him. I let him fuck me. What do you think of that?

I laughed again. For the first time in a long time, it seemed – I was properly laughing. Was it any good? I asked him.

He tensed. You're not shocked?

That you fucked him? No.

He said he was older, but he was, well, he was young. Too young, you know? Then he asked for money – or he'd show my parents photos – show everyone –

He had photos?

Gary rubbed his chin on my hair. It happens a lot here. It's a big thing. A scam. Terrible shame for my mother, my father.

So you paid?

Harris paid.

But do you like boys?

Gary stopped, held me close. After a moment he said, Harris thought he was safe, throwing me at you. Thought I didn't like girls and you – beautiful, with your big eyes and fair hair – would never fall for a fat man –

I don't get it.

I think you do.

So you – well, and then what?

Harris took pity on me. Paid the money to the idiot boy. And offered more – the bookshop. Melly Hill. He made out he'd been living there on and off for years. And then this fucking wonderful coincidence – this ravishing waitress, transforming our lives –

Why didn't you tell me all this? I ask Gary after several minutes have passed and the weight of our gone-away child is still pulling on my heart.

He'd have told you everything –

You cared about that?

At first no, not at all – but then –

Then?

I liked you –

I was a slag, I say.

No, he says, You were so –

211

But even he can't think of the word.

I lick my lips, tasting the darkness and how things have shifted.

What's that clinking? I ask him.

The boats, he sighs. The fishing boats. Panos has three sons. They all fish.

Where are they now?

The sons? They're around.

I haven't seen them.

Amy, he says.

I wriggle because the bed is hard and small like a child's bed. I wonder if God is looking down on all this confessing and laughing. I wonder what the smell is – tallow? Foot sweat? A mosquito whines past.

I felt terrible, lying to you all this time, Gary says.

Moments pass and something has gone, flown past us, and it's not a mosquito.

You've known everything, I tell him, You and Harris. Did you know our baby would die?

I know the answer as I listen to his plain, untouched silence.

I've done more bad things than you have, I say after a while.

I love you, he says. I love you so much it gives me a pain. He said you'd leave me if you knew.

I wouldn't leave you.

I loved Jimmy, he says.

I know. I know you did.

Harris hated me for that, he said and I felt his big body shed more tears.

Are you scared he'll come? I asked him.

Harris? Not now, not at night.

If he comes, what will he do?

I don't know what he's done already. How can I

know what he will do? I don't want him in my life any longer. I don't want him close to you.

I don't want him near Jimmy, I say.

We'll leave here as soon as it's getting light. Are you OK?

I'm fine, I say, but he stays, moving closer, pressing me so tight in his arms I'm almost not breathing. It would be a way to die, wouldn't it – suffocating in the fat man's arms?

I used to like him, I whisper.

I know, he says, pressing his lips down on the top of my head. That wasn't your fault.

I thought – you know – I thought he loved my mother. No one else loved her.

You loved her.

No, I say, I didn't have a chance. I don't think of her with love. I just think of her as a girl, unconnected to me.

Before I can cry, he puts a hand over my mouth, strokes upwards to my damp, hot eyes. I know a place, he whispers, Such a good place for our baby.

He was a miracle, wasn't he? I say, as if my whole life has been pouring towards this moment.

We'll have another one, Gary tells me and I try to explain that there's no space for that in my future, there's no way I could betray Jimmy in that way right now, but I'm wasting my time. He's asleep, breathing his tears into my shoulder.

Later, I move one of his arms off me so I can reach out into the darkness. I pull the bag up easily by its nylon handle, up, on to the bed and across us.

I sleep for the last time with that small weight on me. I want to feel it, want to suffer its weight pressing on me, but I hardly can. It's getting lighter every minute.

*

213

We left in the early dullness of dawn on his moped –
for I found out he could drive a bike just like the rest
of the Greeks, leaning into the corners, planting a foot
casually down into the dust when we stopped.

The roads led upwards, always clouds of dust.
Now and then a patch of cement, then nothing. I
held on to him from behind, he seemed to know the
way.

The bag was between us, pressing my stomach, his
back. It had turned into a small, light thing, hardly
there at all. Gary never mentioned the terrible smell
of our child. Now that we both knew everything, we
found we couldn't speak much.

Faraway now, the sea glittered. You couldn't see
where it stopped and the blueness of the sky took over.

I smelled something else then, cancelling out what
Jimmy had become.

Thyme, said Gary, whipping his head round so I
could hear the words. Thyme, Amy.

It was everywhere, stretching before us, under us,
beyond us.

At first you look and you think you're just seeing rocks
– little grey jutty rocks all over the greenish scrub and
gorse.

Then you force your eyes down and you begin to
make sense of the piles of grey. Fat, broken walls come
at you – half a tower, a roof, an inside of somewhere
with the top blown off. Grey shapes moving out of the
morning, half in, half out of time.

Gary shuts off the bike engine and turns to look at
my face. And the wind drops and my ears feel soft
with nothing.

They built their forts high up on the rocks, he says,
but the pirates still came. Barbarossa sacked the place
and killed everyone – men, women, children. No one

214

ever comes here, not even tourists, because of how haunted it's supposed to be.

I look around me. There are fat daisies growing in the sunshine, different coloured mosses on the greyish rocks, a lizard skittering.

I think it's a beautiful place, I tell him, blinking.

That's because you've been here before.

I've never –

The churches have frescoes in them, he says.

He lays the bike in the grass and takes my hand and I follow, taking the bag, scrambling and shuffling through the papery grass and chamomile and nubble of stones.

The air holds its breath, a coiled thing, meaning us no harm.

We could put him in the church, he says.

He grips on to my hand till it hurts.

We choose the farthest away church with the blackest, slittiest windows and he pulls me and Jimmy in. Straightaway, like she's expecting us, there's fragments of the Virgin's worried face, black with age, hands clasped to her chest. She gabbles her lips at me and shows her teeth – sharp little teeth with gaps. Fear catches at my throat, but Gary grasps my shoulders, holding me still in front of her.

We wait and my heart is bursting.

Then the lights race towards us – dim, bluish-grey – out of the stony dark.

I scream and rush backwards against the grassy wall and all I know is we're out and I'm gulping air.

It's OK, Gary goes, It's OK.

I'm not putting him in there.

OK, says Gary, OK.

Pushing forward through the ruined sunlight.

I don't care about what you did, I tell Gary. You could do anything. You should have known that.

You don't make reasonable judgements when you hate yourself, he says.

I kneel at the bag and unlock the zip for the first time in a great many hours. The silver teeth part, my fingertips touch unavoidable dampness. The sheet has a big, spreading stain, pale brownish, almost not a colour, and my opening it all up naturally stirs up the whiff.

Now Gary sits on a rock, hands over his face, watching me through his fingers.

I make him help me with the circle of stones – two kids playing – and I insist on two layers, safe and tightly overlapping, a small home. I'm the one who lays him in and it's all over easily in a moment. One last, longed-for touching.

Now get some more to cover him, I tell Gary, Smooth ones.

Gary does as I tell him, though none of the rocks are that smooth – their edges are sharp, flecked with shadow.

Not his face, I say, Nothing on his face.

No one ever comes here, he says, because of how frightened he feels.

My heart burns up with loss and grief. I'm frantic not to finish, but I hang over the stiff bundle lying there on the earth and tell him goodbye. Useless words, empty of meaning, but all we have.

I can't leave him, I tell Gary.

He says nothing, then he says, You already have.

We stand there a moment, clenched together in the stillness. Then a sudden burst of movement takes me down and it's over, has long been over and I'm falling on the stones, pulling them off, getting the cloth off of the little body.

216

I wouldn't do that, said Gary but by the time he'd got the words out, it was already done and my fingers were resting in the cloth around his face which was gone, more or less.

The sun was getting warm. Far away there was the sound of a car engine.

The pile of stones looked ordinary now as we moved away. It could have been anything – a run-of-the-mill, private place where a person had had sex or just gone to the toilet.

Don't look back, said Gary and I didn't need to – I already knew that love clung like a shadow to my baby's grave. I was crying so hard the sky had squeezed out of focus. We went down the side of the castle thing and looked over into the gorge – the steepest drop I'd ever seen, making me sick just to look.

Why did Jimmy die? I said, but it was a question for the whole world, not Gary.

When the pirates came, Gary told me, The women threw their children down this ravine. Anything to stop them being sold as slaves.

We left on the moped – dust flying up – just as the sun was getting high.

What if he follows us here? I asked Gary, but he didn't reply. I thought of how many times he hadn't answered my questions.

He'd slung the bag on the handlebars and without it between us, I could hold him tighter, breathe him in for good and for bad.